C000278498

MURDER LUST

A gripping medical thriller

CANDY DENMAN

THE BOOK FOLKS

Paperback edition published by

The Book Folks

London, 2022

© Candy Denman

This book is a work of fiction. Names, characters, businesses, organizations, places and events are either the product of the author's imagination or are used fictitiously. Any resemblance to actual persons, living or dead, events or locales is entirely coincidental. The spelling is British English.

All rights reserved. No part of this publication may be reproduced, stored in retrieval system, copied in any form or by any means, electronic, mechanical, photocopying, recording or otherwise transmitted without written permission from the publisher.

ISBN 978-1-80462-010-6

www.thebookfolks.com

MURDER LUST *is the sixth novel in a series of medical crime fiction titles featuring medical examiner Dr Callie Hughes. More information about the other five books can be found at the end of this one.*

Prologue: The Half-Moon

The more the woman struggled and cried, the more it excited her attackers. Her shirt was torn as she tried to pull away from the man and she cried out, calling for help. He pulled the scarf tighter to stop her noise; they didn't want complaints from the neighbours, he said. That set them both off again. They were laughing so much it was impossible for her to hold the phone still as she filmed it all. That wouldn't do, that wouldn't do at all. It was important to have something to watch later, to remember, to bring back the sheer exhilaration of the moment, to savour it all over again.

Finally, the victim was still, slack, and the photographer moved nearer to get a close-up of her face, blue and swollen like her tongue which stuck out, blood dribbling down her chin where the dead woman had bitten it. She smiled and, putting down the phone she had used to film everything, reached out and stroked the victim's breast. As he watched her, she pressed her fingernail into the flesh hard enough to leave a small half-moon shaped mark despite the gloves she wore, and then turned to him and smiled.

Chapter 1

It wasn't hard to work out which house Callie Hughes was looking for because there was a uniformed police officer standing outside the door. It was a terraced fisherman's cottage, one of nine built around a small patch of shared garden. Callie was glad she'd come on foot; there was absolutely nowhere to park nearby. She was carrying her crime scene bag, containing any equipment she might need, and quickly put on a coverall. Even though it wasn't officially a crime scene yet, she wasn't about to take any chances until she was sure.

As she approached the officer sheltering from the rain under a slight overhang at the front of the cottage, she saw the door had been left slightly ajar. It was an old and solid wood door and there was a key safe attached to the front. This wasn't uncommon, both for holiday lets or for the elderly who might have carers needing access. There was no obvious sign that the door had been forced. Callie smiled at the police officer and gave her name. They hadn't set up a register as yet, he explained, so he simply wrote her name in his notebook.

"Sergeant Maguire's on her way and she said only you and the crime scene techs could go inside, Doctor," he said anxiously.

"That's fine." She smiled encouragement; it was probably his first death. "Who found the body?"

"Cleaner. She's with my partner, giving a statement." He nodded towards the marked car that had pulled up on the pavement a bit further along the road, blue lights flashing a warning and causing a bit of an obstruction and much muttering and rubbernecking from motorists trying to pass by.

"Right," she said. "I'll go in and take a look."

Adjusting her mask, putting on gloves and pulling up the hood on her crime scene coveralls, Callie made sure that all her blonde hair was tucked inside before entering the cottage. She awkwardly stooped and pulled on bootees as she crossed the threshold, careful not to bring any mud or rainwater inside.

The door led into a tiny hallway with just enough room to hang coats on the row of three hooks. Callie noted that there was only one coat hanging there and a pair of trainers carefully placed underneath.

She did not take the most direct route through the room, conscious that there might be footprints that could be recovered and not wanting to be the one who had scuffed them. It was a comfortable, homely sitting room, with its large fireplace containing a log burner. Lots of bright watercolours, mostly of fish and seashells, adorned the walls. Two wingback chairs were positioned to get the best of the heat from the fireplace, whilst the dining table and two chairs were by the small window. She continued through to the tiny but well-equipped kitchen, where a back door was still bolted, top and bottom, and then she moved on up the stairs at the back of the house, stepping to either side of each tread. A quick glance out of the window showed a neat patio garden, with wrought-iron chairs and a matching table for outdoor dining, should the rain ever stop.

At the top of the steep, creaky stairs, there were two open doorways. One led into a surprisingly spacious bathroom, the other to a double bedroom. In the dim light filtering through the heavy curtains, Callie could see the bottom half of a woman's bare legs on the bed and, taking a deep breath, she entered the room.

The young woman was lying on her back, hair splayed out across the pillow like a fan, both hands up by her neck. She was fully dressed apart from shoes, but her cream blouse looked to have been torn open, revealing her lacy bra. Callie could see a button, still attached to a bit of fabric, on the floor, and another button was still hanging on, but only by a thread. The shirt could have been torn deliberately or in a struggle perhaps. Her jeans were still on and fully done up.

Callie didn't realise she had been holding her breath until she let it go. At least it didn't look like a sexual assault. Callie leaned forward and felt for a carotid pulse. As expected, it was not there. Even through her gloves, the skin was cold to the touch, and the woman's still open eyes were cloudy. Callie reached for a hand and lifted it up; there was resistance, so rigor mortis was at least partially present. She had been dead for some time and Callie didn't need her training to tell her that the bruised neck and protruding tongue meant that this wasn't a case of death by natural causes. She was about to leave when she noticed a small mark on the woman's partly exposed breast. She photographed it on her phone, making a note to mention it in her report to the pathologist so that it could be swabbed for DNA. There was nothing more she could do here, it was time to call in the troops.

Chapter 2

Callie was waiting outside the house, holding an umbrella over her head in a vain attempt to keep dry as she watched Colin Brewer, the crime scene manager, bustling about and issuing orders. He was organising the technicians, uniformed police officers, and, of course, the scene. He wanted a larger perimeter for his investigators to work within and that meant effectively closing the road, much to the anger of some of the motorists who were being sent on a lengthy diversion. Sergeant Maguire, much as she might want to argue, knew that wasn't going to work and was instead turning her attention, and sharp tongue, on the drivers who dared to complain.

Colin Brewer was a short, stocky man, with thick, steel-grey hair and an ex-military air about him, and there was no denying he was the best crime scene manager that Callie had ever worked with. She was thankful that it was him who was in charge here this morning and that Sergeant Maguire was being so assertive in ensuring the scene was not compromised.

She glanced at her watch and wondered how her patients were getting on. She had rushed out of morning surgery as soon as the call came in, leaving Linda

Crompton, the practice manager, organising new appointments for them later in the week if they could wait, or fitting them in with other doctors if they couldn't. This was a regular occurrence, and if her colleagues couldn't be described as happy to take on the extra work her call-outs engendered, at least they didn't make too much fuss. Thankfully Callie had seen the bulk of her morning list before the call had come in. Juggling her two part-time jobs, as a GP and as a forensic physician with the police, was hard work – for Callie, her colleagues, and for her patients in particular.

Despite the persistent light rain, Callie had removed her crime scene coveralls, well aware that they did no one any favours, and tried to straighten her shoulder-length blonde hair, pulling it back into a ponytail, whilst juggling with the umbrella. She knew Detective Inspector Steve Miller was on his way, and much as she didn't need, or want, to impress him, she couldn't help herself doing it.

"Watcha, Doc!"

Callie tried not to jump, or let her face fall as she saw Detective Sergeant Bob Jeffries walking up the road. Short, with skinny arms and legs and more than a hint of a paunch, his once ginger hair almost white, Miller's sidekick looked as if he had just rolled out of bed and thrown yesterday's clothes on. Which, to be fair, he probably had. Further along the road, she could see Detective Inspector Steve Miller. Tall and dark-haired, he had the rugged good looks of someone who has lived an interesting life and she felt a slight flutter in her stomach. She had never worked out whether it was attraction or irritation that caused it. He showed absolutely no interest in her and was staring at his phone with great intensity as he followed his sergeant.

Callie acknowledged Jeffries' greeting with a nod as she watched his boss flick through something on his phone with a grin on his face. She was sure there was something different about him, but couldn't quite put her finger on it. He certainly seemed to have got over his recent divorce; he no longer looked haunted or stressed and his hair was different.

"How's it going, Steve?" she asked and he looked up, guiltily, and hastily tucked his phone in his pocket.

"Good, thanks," he said quickly, before looking at the house where a constable now stood with a proper clipboard, noting everyone going in or out and the times. "What have we got?" He turned the collar of his jacket up, to try and prevent too much rain going down his neck.

"Young woman, thirties, fully dressed, signs of a struggle, bruising to her neck, small mark on her breast, no other injuries that I could see. First sight suggests strangulation. There's a degree of rigor, so we're probably talking between two and twenty-four hours ago but they may be able to tell you more after the PM." Although Callie knew that it was unlikely that they would be able to bring the window of time down to anything less than a few hours, they would at least know if rigor was just setting in, or beginning to go.

"Fully dressed, you said?"

She nodded.

"Yes, although her blouse was ripped." Callie sniffed and wrinkled her nose. There was a sweet, musky smell in the air and she wondered what it was. Definitely not Miller's usual sandalwood scent; surely DS Jeffries hadn't taken to wearing aftershave?

Miller interrupted her thoughts. "Does it look like she could have been redressed afterwards?"

"I don't think so." Callie had learned the hard way early on in her career not to rule anything out, but there had been nothing to suggest that was what had happened.

Colin Brewer came over to join them and update Miller on progress with the crime scene.

"Mortuary van's on its way and we should be able to move the body soon."

It was a gentle hint that if they wanted to see the crime scene with the body in situ, they needed to get a move on.

As Miller and Jeffries hurried off to get into their protective suits Callie turned to Brewer.

"Anything interesting so far?"

"Nope. Of course, there might have been if the cleaner hadn't already done the downstairs before going up and finding the body. At least she hadn't cleaned the ruddy bathroom yet."

He turned and went back into the house and followed the now suited and booted detectives through the door. He wouldn't want to let them just wander around the house on their own; he'd need to be there, just to be sure they didn't touch anything.

Callie decided there was nothing more she could do at the house and that she would be better occupied getting back to her day job and catching up on any patients still to be seen. As it was technically her half day and she didn't have an evening surgery, she would be able to smooth things over with her colleagues by taking more than her fair share of visits as well. She hurried along the road to the steps leading down to George Street.

Chapter 3

Once her bumper list of visits was finished, Callie decided to drop into the mortuary before going home. She hadn't been since Billy Iqbal, the last pathologist, had left for his new post in Northern Ireland and she wondered how she would feel being there, and how the place would have changed with someone else in charge. There had been quite a few pathologists in the time she had been a forensic physician in the town, but none she had cared for as much as Billy.

She walked along the corridor and was surprised to hear music coming from one of the rooms. To be fair, it wasn't loud, and the first pathologist she had known in Hastings had often played classical music as he worked, but this definitely wasn't classical. She paused to listen; it was Pink Floyd, if she wasn't very much mistaken. She opened the door and found Jim, the mortuary technician, laying out instruments.

"Another brick in the wall," he sang and banged some forceps against the trolley in time with the music.

"Hello, Jim," she called out, loud enough to be heard above the music.

He looked up and grinned at her, revealing the appalling condition of the few teeth he had left.

"Hi, Doc, you've finally come to meet Matt, have you?"

She ignored the implied rebuke. "Is he in?"

"Office," Jim replied and went back to his work, singing along as he did so. "We don't need no…"

Callie went back out to the corridor to Billy's office, or Matt's office, as she would have to get used to calling it.

If there was a change to the feel of the mortuary – more relaxed, more music – there had been a seismic change in the style of the office. As there was no one in the room, Callie took a moment to look around. It didn't take long as the room was tiny. Meticulously tidy in Billy's day, it wasn't exactly messy now, but it was full of things everywhere you looked. Actually, Callie thought, it was a mess. There wasn't a surface anywhere in the room that wasn't covered with pictures, forms, official-looking letters and books, and nothing was quite lined up straight. There were pieces of paper on the desk, a tray of more pieces of paper, a half-full coffee cup sitting next to a coaster which had a happy family photo on it, and a coffee ring next to that, showing that the pathologist liked to put his cup down on anything but the coaster. Perhaps he didn't like to disrespect his family by covering them up.

A luridly painted, hand-made pencil pot, that might have been meant to be a teddy bear, contained one chewed pen and teetered dangerously close to the edge of the desk. There were several pictures on the wall as well as pinned to the corkboard amongst the list of phone extensions and reminders of meetings. Most were of children or done by children. Callie leant closer to one family group: a man in his thirties, smiling proudly, a woman with rainbow-coloured hair next to him and three children, two boys and a girl, all young.

"That's Laura, my wife, and the three rug rats are Jack, Alex and the littlest is Peach," a voice said behind her, and Callie turned to see the man in the photo.

She stood back to let him in the room; he was bigger than Billy, tall and well-built, so this was easier said than done in the very small room. He finally managed to get past her and slid behind the desk.

"Hi, I'm Dr Hughes, Callie, the local—"

"Police doctor," he finished for her.

"Well, yes, and a GP too."

"Of course. I'm Matt Baxter." He looked as if he might hold out his hand but them changed his mind. People didn't do that anymore, not since Covid. "Please take a seat."

Callie pulled up a stool, moving the files on it and putting them on top of a filing cabinet, unable to resist closing the gaping drawers as she did so.

"How are you settling in?" she asked to cover the moment of awkwardness that followed.

"Just fine, thanks. It's a good unit and Jim is worth his weight in gold."

"I'm glad he's decided to stay."

"Me too, let me tell you, it's bad enough getting used to a new hospital without having to break in new staff as well."

"I'm sure. What brought you to Hastings?" she asked.

"My wife's family is from round here, and we've always visited often, loved it, so it made sense."

"It's nice that you have roots here."

"So, I'm likely to stay?" He smiled. "Yes, I heard that there have been a few different pathologists over the past few years, and I know you must have been sad that your, um, friend, left to further his career."

"You've no plans like that yourself?" she asked, hoping that it wasn't a rude question.

"Not at all, I'm perfectly happy doing the more, well, mundane work. Office hours and home in time to put the kids to bed, that's what I want." He looked pointedly at his watch and she realised she had better get down to business as it was approaching six o'clock.

"Do you know what's happening with the woman I saw this morning?"

"She was taken to Brighton for her PM. You'll have to talk to them, I'm afraid, I somehow doubt they'll bother keeping me in the loop."

He seemed quite happy about that and she reflected on the change. Billy would have been fuming at the thought of not knowing what was going on, not being involved, but Matt was perfectly okay with it. If there was one word that seemed to sum him up, it was 'content'. He was contented with his lot in life.

Things had certainly changed in the mortuary.

* * *

"So, what's all this I hear about a murder?" Kate Ward leaned forward, eager to hear. "Come on, tell me all."

They were in the snug bar of the The Stag Inn, their favourite pub in Hastings Old Town. Kate was Callie's best friend and confidante. She was a local solicitor, specialising in criminal work, and joked that they had many clients in common – live ones, that is. Callie would see them in the custody suite at the police station, checking that they were fit for interview in the cases where people were drunk, drugged or unwell, and Kate would represent them, advising them to make no comments in interview. It worked well, except in the domestic violence cases. Kate found it very hard representing men who had inflicted sometimes horrific injuries, meticulously catalogued by Callie. Kate would have much preferred to be prosecuting these men rather than trying to defend their actions, but they both knew she wouldn't last long in the Crown Prosecution Service; she was much too independent.

They were opposites, in both character and physical appearance. Kate was full-bodied and dark-haired, and favoured bright, jewel-coloured, floaty clothing, whereas Callie was blonde, slim, and elegantly dressed in tailored pastel shades. They made a striking pair.

Callie took a sip of her white wine and looked around, checking no one was listening in to their conversation before answering, quietly.

"Young woman staying in rented holiday accommodation."

"I know that much from Minna."

"Minna?" Callie asked.

"Minna Nowak. The owner. She's a local artist who earns a bit of money on the side renting out her home."

That explained all the paintings Callie had seen dotted around the house.

"And she got the details from the cleaner who found the body?"

"Minna couldn't afford a cleaner!" Kate laughed before explaining, "It was her who found the woman. She was really shocked, I can tell you."

"That's not surprising."

"Was it as grim as she told me?"

"Yes and no. It wasn't pleasant. There's not much more I can tell you until the results of the post-mortem are in."

Kate knew very well that her friend wouldn't divulge any details before she was supposed to, it was more than her job was worth, and the questions were only a tease. Not to say that she wouldn't have really liked to know more and, much as she admired her friend for her professionalism, it was a source of great frustration for her.

"Is the house Minna's main home?" Callie was, of course, free to question her friend to get more details, even if the reverse wasn't true.

"Yes, she moves out when she gets a booking, goes and stays with her mother over in Bexhill."

"Presumably she's been able to give the police the woman's details then?"

"I'm sure she has," Kate replied. "Hopefully they'll be able to contact her next of kin."

Not a job either of them envied.

"Does Minna know who she was staying down here with? Husband? Boyfriend?" Callie knew most murders were committed by someone close to the victim, but she couldn't remember if she had seen a wedding ring when she checked the body. The killer could have been another woman, of course, but it would have to have been someone pretty strong to hold the young woman down and strangle her like that, so Callie was willing to bet that it had been a man.

Kate drank some more of her cloudy pale ale and shook her head.

"No, she only has the details that came through from the booking site. She finds it easier not to get to know the renters, particularly if there are complaints, on either side. Although she has a few regulars that she deals with directly."

Callie could imagine it was easier to keep the relationship strictly professional.

"I'd hate to think of strangers in my home," she said.

"Me too," Kate replied. "I don't think Minna's that happy about it either, but it's better than having to get a regular job which might eat into her painting time."

"And her mother doesn't mind her coming to stay so often?"

"I rather think she'd like Minna to move in permanently and look after her, but she's a difficult woman, by all accounts, and Minna needs her own space, just to get a break every now and then."

Callie could understand that. She got on much better with her own mother from a distance.

"How's Diego?" Callie asked, hoping she had got the name of Kate's current squeeze right. She had met him a couple of weeks before, just briefly, and although he was undoubtedly handsome, his ego had needed far too much stroking for her liking.

"Oh, you know, okay I suppose."

"Well, that's hardly an endorsement. What's wrong?"

"Just a lover's tiff." Kate smiled. "Don't worry, we'll sort it out."

Callie hoped they did; Kate had seemed quite taken by him only the week before and although Callie didn't rate him, Kate had even talked about the possibility of him moving in with her at some point.

"Are you going to see Billy this weekend?" Kate asked her, changing the subject away from her own love life.

"No, he's at a conference in Vienna and I'm on call." What with her duties both as a GP and as a police doctor and Billy's new job as a pathologist in Belfast, they were finding it hard to see each other as often as they liked. Long-distance relationships were always difficult to sustain, even with all the different types of communication available in this day and age. There was no substitute for actually being together and Callie, once again, rued the ambition that had taken Billy away from Hastings and her bed.

"Did you happen to see Detective Inspector Miller at the scene, by any chance?" Kate was grinning mischievously as she said this, knowing that Callie's feelings towards the man were distinctly mixed.

"Yes," Callie admitted, "but there was something strange about him, though. Something different."

She thought for a few moments, recalling him walking up the road, preoccupied by his mobile phone, a smile playing on his lips.

"His hair!" she exclaimed. "He's done something different with his hair. Cut his fringe shorter and spiked it up with some sort of product. Gel or mousse or something, and he's changed his aftershave to something pretty potent, not to mention revolting." Callie had always loved the smell of soap and sandalwood that usually emanated from the detective inspector. What on earth had induced him to change it?

"Aaah." Kate grinned. "My money's on a new girlfriend."

And Callie knew that she was probably right.

Chapter 4

Callie leant back and closed her eyes for a moment. She had just finished a morning surgery that had seemed to go on forever. She knew it was because she was catching up with some of the patients she had let down the day before when she had been called out to the crime scene, but it was still a long one, by anyone's standards. There had been a couple of complaints from people who had had to wait, but most of her regulars knew the score and that she would fit them in when she could or they could see one of her colleagues if it was urgent.

There was a knock on the door and Callie was startled awake.

"Come in!" she called, quickly checking the time on her watch as the computer screen seemed to have gone to sleep, like her. She was pleased to see that she had only slept for a few minutes.

Linda Crompton came into the room, holding a plastic basket of papers. Callie groaned.

Linda smiled as she put the basket on Callie's desk and went back out to pick up the tray she had placed outside the door.

"Coffee and a chicken salad sandwich," she said as she put the tray down. "Just what the doctor ordered."

"Well, I have to agree, but I don't remember ordering it." Callie frowned. "Is there a practice meeting or something?"

"No, but I didn't want to give you the chance to go out gallivanting before you tackled your paperwork and picked up your visit list. I know what you're like."

Linda knew her too well and she was absolutely right. Callie was itching to get over to the police station to see if the initial results of the post-mortem were back, and to hear whether the victim's next of kin had been contacted, not to mention finding out what Colin had to say about the crime scene. Had there been signs of a break-in she hadn't spotted, or, as Callie suspected, was the murderer someone the victim knew? Someone she let into the house? Or even someone she was staying with?

Giving a small sigh, Callie turned to look at the basket of papers. She knew she would have to sort through it and tackle all the urgent requests, but at least she didn't have to find time to get lunch as well, thanks to Linda. She bit into her sandwich and started on the pile.

* * *

It was almost three o'clock before Callie finally managed to get to the police station. She made her way upstairs to where an incident room ought to have been set up by now. To her surprise, the open-plan room was not the hive of activity she had expected. Instead of extra desks being set up and civilian staff manning phone lines, the room was unusually quiet.

Detective Sergeant Jayne Hales, in her late thirties and a motherly figure in her comfortable office wear and flat shoes, looked up as Callie entered the room, and quickly glanced over her shoulder. Callie could see that she was looking at the small office, separated from the room by nothing more than a rather flimsy plasterboard wall that gave Steve Miller the illusion of privacy. The door was shut, but Callie could see Steve and Bob Jeffries in there. They seemed to be arguing over something. No change there, then.

"Hi Jayne," Callie said.

"Hiya — the boss is a bit busy at the moment." She seemed nervous and checked over her shoulder again. Miller and Jeffries were still quietly, but forcefully, talking and Jeffries wasn't looking happy. "Do you fancy a coffee?" Jayne asked.

Callie was about to refuse, knowing how grim the coffee in the station could be, when the detective added, "The café down the road does a decent cappuccino."

Callie nodded her agreement. A café was a different matter entirely and Jayne clearly wanted to speak to her outside the station; she was already grabbing her bag and heading for the door. Callie followed, wondering what on earth was going on.

* * *

The café was probably not one Callie would have entered under normal circumstances. It specialised in fry-ups and Callie could almost see the grease running down the walls, complemented, or rather not, by the smell of stale cooking oil and sweat. There were copies of The Sun and the Daily Mail in a rack by the door, and Callie recognised most of the current clientele from the police station. Both sides of the law frequented the place, it seemed, which made sense given its proximity.

Whilst they were waiting in a queue to give their orders, Callie and Jayne kept to general chit-chat. Had she seen Billy recently? Jayne asked. As the local pathologist, Billy had been known by many of the police officers and was well liked by them all. Callie hoped they didn't blame her for him upping sticks and moving to Belfast. After all, she hadn't wanted him to go either, but with no vacancies for Home Office pathologists this side of the water, there was little choice if he wanted to progress his career. She had always known that Hastings was too much of a backwater to keep someone as ambitious as Billy for long. Callie changed the subject by asking about Jayne's husband and children. She could only imagine how organised Jayne had to be to manage both a very demanding job and bringing up three children. Rumour had it that her husband wasn't much help with either.

Once they were settled at a corner table with their coffees, Jayne checked no one was close enough to overhear. The general noise levels in the place, with the crashing of crockery and cutlery and the hiss of steam from the tea urn, meant she didn't have to worry too much. Jayne took a sip of her coffee and sighed.

"Thanks, I really needed to get out of there."

"Why? What's up?" Callie asked.

Jayne hesitated.

"The atmosphere seemed a little, um, tense," Callie prompted.

"Tense doesn't even begin to cover it," Jayne replied, with feeling. "I've never known it to be so bad, not since DI Miller came, anyway."

"What's the reason?"

"The boss, well, he—" Jayne still seemed a little unsure about telling Callie what was going on. She fiddled with her cup and Callie waited. "He wants to hand the case over to the Met," she said finally.

Callie was too shocked to say anything, not that Jayne gave her the chance. Having started to tell Callie what was going on, there was no stopping her.

"The victim was from London, you see. Just came down for a two-day stay in the town. There was no sign of a break-in so the boss reckons that the killer was someone who came down with her. He thinks that it's a domestic that has its roots in London so they should be the lead investigators, and the superintendent agrees."

"What?" Callie was as shocked as Jayne. She would have laid money on Steve fighting to keep the case. After all, the murder had happened here, even if the business had started in London.

"I know, I know, it's so unlike him to give it up so easily."

"And the superintendent?"

"Oh, he's happy with anything that will save money. He's sold it to the chief on the grounds that we don't have the budget for the extra manpower a murder enquiry would need."

They were both silent for a minute, drinking their coffee, which Callie had to admit wasn't bad, and processing Miller's change of attitude.

"Why do you think he's doing this?" Callie finally asked.

Jayne looked shifty and wriggled in her seat like a child caught cheating at school.

"Come on, Jayne, you can tell me," Callie encouraged her.

"Well, you know he's got a new girlfriend, right?"

"I'd spotted the new haircut and guessed," Callie said, without mentioning that it was actually Kate who had called it.

Jayne looked relieved.

"Honestly, he's besotted with the woman. He's like a teenager and he hasn't got the brain space, or the energy, to think about anything else."

"I take it Bob Jeffries doesn't approve."

"Understatement of the year. He very nearly blew a gasket when he heard about giving the case to the Met."

Callie could imagine the scene; whatever else, Bob Jeffries was fiercely territorial. He was also very loyal to his boss, so he must be torn.

"What's she like, this new girlfriend?"

"No idea. None of us has actually met the woman. We just know that he's late in most mornings, and among the first to leave, and he's pretty useless in between times because he's always on his ruddy phone, texting her, or sexting, I expect."

Callie was shocked. She knew Steve Miller had been through some difficult times, but he had always maintained his professionalism, always put the job first – well, almost always. It's what had cost him his marriage. His wife had lost their baby and blamed him because he was "never there for her". Unable to forgive, she had finally divorced him a year ago.

"So, what happens next?" Callie asked.

"There's a couple of detectives on their way down from London now. The boss is going to brief them once they arrive and then formally hand over the case."

Callie tried to think of something she could say to cheer Jayne up, but, for once, she was lost for words.

Chapter 5

On her way back to the surgery, Callie called in to a care home up on The Ridge.

As she parked her car in one of the visitor spaces in front of the imposing Victorian building, she couldn't help wondering if it had been planned that way or if it was just a coincidence that the home, named Glenalmond, was situated so close to the cemetery. It smacked of hurrying the residents towards their final destination and she couldn't believe that it didn't put a few people off coming to the place.

Like many residential care facilities, the house had originally belonged to a wealthy family and was sold after the war to be used as a private school which had only closed twenty years ago. It had taken extensive refurbishing to make the house suitable for the current use and it had been a shining example of a homely, comfortable place for those who lived there. But that had been when it was newly opened and when money was less scarce for those relying on local authority funds. Callie knew that the home now didn't get enough from the council to cover the cost of the care it provided, and that the very few private residents in the place had to pay more to make up for the shortfall.

Anything that could be cut to save money, was, and there were regular fundraising events because the home was constantly running at a loss. The vicious circle so many care homes faced was that the less that was spent on keeping the place looking nice, the fewer private residents chose them, and their income reduced still further. Looking up at the outside of the building, Callie could see that it was beginning to look a little tired. It was clear that the owners probably didn't have as much spare cash to spend on upkeep as they would wish. The grass was in need of a trim and there were more weeds than flowers in the beds either side of the front door, suggesting that the gardener's hours had been cut, or possibly that he or she had gone entirely.

With a slight feeling of guilt, Callie realised that it had been some time since her last visit to the home. She had two patients who lived there and she was only calling now because one of them had been taken to A&E after a fall. The hospital summary stated that Barbara Conway had sustained a broken clavicle and bruising to her ribs and had been discharged back to the nursing home for ongoing care. The summary also made the point that this was the third time Mrs Conway had been seen in the emergency department in as many months, although the injuries this time were the most severe.

Callie walked up to the front door and rang the bell. Gone were the days when she would have been able to walk straight in and see her patient. An elderly man with dementia had walked out of another care home a few years back and got himself run over on the bypass. His legacy was better security in every facility in the locality. Some residents, and their families, felt safer for these measures but others complained it was like being in prison. You could never please everyone.

At last Callie heard footsteps and the door was opened by a middle-aged woman in a blue uniform with a badge declaring her name as Carol and her title as Matron. The uniform and the title were meant to make you think Carol was a nurse even though Callie knew she wasn't really, but she had never heard any complaints about the way Carol ran the home.

"Dr Hughes, come in. We are expecting you."

Callie followed her into the large hall. With its tall ceilings, polished wood floors and an enormous display of high-quality imitation flowers on a side table, the room was meant to impress visitors and potential residents, and it did.

"I'm here to see Mrs Conway, Matron."

"Of course, poor dear."

The matron led the way through a maze of corridors and up a flight of stairs at a brisk pace, talking as she did so. There was an overriding smell of air freshener, masking goodness only knows what. Callie sniffed. Cabbage? Urine? A mixture of both?

"She fell in the night, taking herself to the loo again."

"Doesn't she need help to do that?"

"Well, yes, but you know how confused they can get," Carol replied in a conspiratorial whisper. "She should have rung for help, but she didn't. We put cot sides on her bed after the last time she took a tumble in the night, but she just climbed over them."

They stopped outside a door and the matron knocked and went in without waiting for a reply. "Doctor's here to see you, Barbie, and I've been telling her about you being naughty."

Callie winced at the shortening of the poor woman's name. She didn't think Mrs Conway would like to be referred to in that way or the patronising suggestion that she was being naughty. She followed the matron into a bright and cheerful room. There was an empty hospital-style bed in the centre, with the cot sides raised. A bit like shutting the stable door after the horse has bolted, Callie thought. Mrs Conway was sitting in an upright wipe-clean chair to one side of the bed and was trapped firmly in place by an adjustable bedside table. She was dressed in an easy-wash dress and comfy slippers. Her hair had been done and the call buzzer was placed within reach on the table in front of her, along with a plastic beaker of tea. She looked well cared for, apart from her arm being in a cross-body sling, and some visible bruises to her legs and face.

"You have to push the call button if you need anything, don't you, Barbie?" Carol was talking loudly and clearly. Callie didn't think Mrs Conway was deaf, but perhaps the matron had got into the habit of talking to everyone in the home like that.

"Hello, Mrs Conway," Callie said and pulled over a footstool to sit on and bring herself down to Mrs Conway's level. "How are you feeling today?"

"Not very well, Doctor. I fell over," she replied, holding up the arm that was in a sling and grimacing with pain as she did so.

"I know. Try not to move the arm if you can help it – we want your collarbone to mend."

Mrs Conway nodded her understanding.

"The hospital said you also bruised your ribs, is that right?"

"Yes, but they're not broken."

"No, but I bet it still hurts to breathe, doesn't it?"

"Yes, it does, and when I try and move."

"Is it okay if I have a listen to your chest?" Callie opened her medical bag and took out a stethoscope.

Carol helped unzip her patient's dress so that she could listen to her breathing from the back, and then she pulled it down slightly at the front to listen there. Callie was shocked by the bruising, it was a wonder that Mrs Conway hadn't broken a rib. The patches were a deep red now, but they would be all shades of the rainbow over the coming days and weeks.

"Well, the good news is your chest is clear, but I'll pop in later in the week to check again and see how you're doing. Meanwhile, no more getting out of bed on your own." Callie stood up and put her stethoscope away.

"I don't like to bother the nurses."

"It's what they're there for," Carol chided her as she straightened the table and made sure the bell was back within reach before ushering Callie out of the room.

"I don't know what we can do to make sure she stays in bed at night, I really don't."

"Is she okay in the day? Does she wander? Seem confused?" Callie asked as they walked along the corridor passing the lift. The doors were wedged open with a trolley piled with clean laundry, so they headed for the stairs.

"No, not really. We bring her down to the dayroom for an hour or so in the morning and for tea later in the afternoon. She likes to watch the quiz shows on television. It's only at night that she's a bother."

"Well, keep an eye on her, I'm worried about her getting a chest infection. Those bruises are bound to stop her from breathing too deeply."

As she walked to her car, Callie took a deep breath of fresh air. What would she do if one, or both, of her parents needed care in the future? There was no escaping the fact that they weren't getting any younger, even if they were fit and well for now. Callie knew she would do everything in her power to keep them at home for as long as possible. Even if that meant getting a live-in carer. So long as that carer wasn't her. Her parents would hate it, she told herself, and, like Kate's friend Minna, she needed her own space.

* * *

Finally, back in her own flat after a long and busy day, Callie kicked off her shoes by the door, placed her bag down beside them and hung up her coat. Her home was the top flat of three in a house high up on the East Hill, overlooking Hastings Old Town and the seafront. The view from the large front window had sold the flat to Callie. That, and the luxury of a parking space, something that was as rare as hen's teeth in the area. She loved her morning commute to the surgery on a fine day: a walk across the country park and down the steps to Rock-a-Nore. Of course, it wasn't quite so nice going back up if the lift wasn't working or if it was raining, but the lack of parking at the surgery meant she usually did walk to work, and told herself it was better than a workout at the gym.

The spacious living area of the flat was open plan, with only a breakfast bar separating the kitchen area from the rest of the room. Standing behind it and filling the kettle, Callie thought about what to have for dinner. Back when Billy was around, he would often come and cook for her. There was no doubt he was better at it than she would ever be, and she missed his Thai green curry almost as much as she missed him. At least she had lost weight since he left. Every cloud…

A brief check of the fridge told her there were few options inside, and certainly nothing that excited her, so she turned to the freezer compartment and took out a ready meal. Vegetarian lasagne would have to do; she just hoped the leftover salad in the fridge was still edible enough to go with it.

While the lasagne was defrosting she made herself a cup of Lady Grey tea, and carried it through to the living room. She would ring Billy after she had eaten. They spoke every day, but it wasn't the same as seeing him and she was looking forward to a planned trip to Ireland in a couple of weeks. When he had left earlier in the year, they had agreed to alternate weekends in Belfast and Hastings, but with both of them juggling on-call rotas, it hadn't proved as easy as that.

Callie sipped her tea and picked up the television remote control. She was too late for the early evening news, but she could watch the news channel and see if anything momentous had happened during the day. She discovered quite quickly that the answer was no.

The microwave pinged, and Callie settled down to a quiet evening meal before calling Billy.

"I've finally met the new pathologist," she told him, when he answered her call.

"You took your time. What's he like?"

"Nice. Family man, pictures of children all over the place."

"I've heard good things about him. He's dependable, hard working, knows what he's doing."

"That's my impression too."

"And I've also heard he's not overly ambitious. He'll stick around."

"Yes, it will be good to get some continuity going."

There were a few moments of embarrassed silence, with both of them wondering what it would have been like if Billy had been the same, before he pointedly changed the subject.

"I thought we could go to the Giant's Causeway when you come over," he told her. "Maybe stay up there and do some of the coastal walk if it's not raining too hard. I'll look for a B&B."

She knew he was trying to make her at least like Northern Ireland, if not fall in love with it, in an effort to persuade her to come over and join him, but he knew the weather was never going to be a draw. Whenever she spoke to him, and certainly on the few occasions she had been over to see him, it always seemed to be raining. She sighed and looked out of the rain-streaked window; there was quite enough rain in Hastings. It was a pity Billy hadn't moved somewhere sunny. That said, she couldn't imagine leaving her home, her family and her friends and moving anywhere. Even for Billy.

The Beginning

How had it all started? At first, when the sex had become routine, boring, they experimented with simple things to spice things up like watching porn, taking photographs of each other, and then unsuspecting victims in changing rooms and upskirting. Then they moved on to more violent porn, experimenting with S&M, even using scarves to cut off their air at the moment of orgasm, but the thrill always wore off and they needed to find more ways, different ways of getting to the same level of excitement. That was when they started exploring the Kama Sutra, not just trying the positions but the touching and biting too, and then they had the idea of doing it not just on each other, but on anonymous victims too, but it wasn't easy.

The first time they succeeded they were staying at a holiday cottage in Hastings when they found themselves in an unexpected crowd. It was the annual Jack-in-the-Green festival and all the locals and a fair few tourists were filling the streets. As a procession went past, there was a crush of people pushing forward and she found herself pushed up against the man in front, sideways on, her pubic bone against his hand. With a sly smile at her partner she rubbed herself against the hand. The man looked startled when he realised what was going on, and tried to move his hand away, but then he realised she seemed to be enjoying it, and he changed.

He moved his hand further against the flimsy cotton of her dress, realising that she was wearing nothing underneath, and then stuck his fingers between her legs with a leer. She seemed to be enjoying it so he was surprised when she grabbed his hand and raked it with her nails. He pulled back, and she screamed and went to try and slap him. Then her partner, her lover, leapt forward and punched the man in the face. He went down like a sack of bricks, head hitting the pavement with a sickening crunch.

The crowd pulled away from them, turning to see what had happened. It seemed it was more interesting than the celebrations in front. Some police community support officers were pushing their way through the heaving mass of people, trying to see what the commotion was all about. They ran.

As soon as they were safely out of sight, in an alley away from the crowds, they stopped to catch their breath. He grabbed her and kissed her, they were laughing and kissing and excited. He pulled her dress up.

"You dirty whore! Letting him grope you, like that," he said as he undid his trousers and pulled his cock free.

They had urgent, frantic, rough, sex there, in that alley, up against the wall. This was the first time she marked someone and the first time they had used violence against others as an aphrodisiac, but it was not to be the last.

Chapter 6

It was an unusual luxury for Callie to have a Saturday morning to herself and she was making the most of it. With visiting Billy in Belfast and being on call so often, either for the surgery or the police, she knew it might be a while before she had the chance of another lie-in. She took a cup of tea back to bed and after that had a leisurely bath and was still in her dressing-gown when the front door bell rang. She mentally checked that she wasn't expecting visitors or a delivery as she clicked the intercom by the door.

"Hello?"

"Erm, it's me. DS Jeffries," a disembodied voice replied. The system distorted it slightly, but even so, he sounded uncertain of who he was, or why he was there.

She buzzed him in, automatically saying, "Top floor," which was totally unnecessary as it wasn't that long since he had last been there, on the dreadful night that Billy got stabbed. Leaving her own flat door open for him, she hurried to her bedroom to throw on some clothes. As she pulled on her jeans, she hoped he was as hesitant coming up the two flights of stairs as he had sounded over the intercom, she didn't want him arriving before she was dressed.

Clothes on and a quick check in the mirror that she was neat and decent, Callie hurried back out into her living room, just as Jeffries peered round her front door.

"Morning," he said, then checked his watch to make sure it still was. If possible, he looked more rumpled than usual, and dejected. He was definitely wearing yesterday's dress shirt, without a tie, and he was unshaven. He looked as if he had been running his hands through his short grey hair all night because it was standing up in various different directions.

"Cup of tea?" she asked brightly, grabbing the kettle as she went to the sink and trying not to sound too out of breath.

"Please."

"Have a seat." She waved towards the sofa and chairs and he did as he was told, while she placed two mugs of tea, a milk jug and a sugar bowl on a tray and brought it over.

"This is, well, unexpected," she said once she had handed him his mug and watched with a raised eyebrow as he spooned three sugars into it and stirred vigorously.

"For us both."

"Is everything all right?" she asked, suddenly anxious that he had come to break bad news — but surely he would have brought Miller or a family liaison officer if it was her parents, or Billy.

He hesitated.

"Is Steve okay?" she asked.

"Well, that is the million-dollar question, isn't it?" he replied cryptically and Callie realised what his visit was all about.

"I take it Steve doesn't know what you're doing? That you've come to see me?"

"Too bloody right, he doesn't. And he'd have a fit if he knew." He put his cup down. "Look, this isn't right. I shouldn't be here." He stood.

"Sit down, Bob. I won't tell him you've been here, and I'm as upset as you. Well, maybe not quite so much, but I am still at a loss to know why he would hand over the case to the Met."

Maybe it was surprise at her using his first name, when she only ever referred to him as Sergeant – or Detective Sergeant Jeffries when she was particularly irritated by him and his attitudes – but he did as he was told and sat down.

"He's obsessed by this, this—" He looked up, stopping himself from make a derogatory remark about the woman his boss was seeing.

"Obsessed is a strong word."

"Yeah, well, perhaps it's more that he seems to have lost interest in everything else. His work, his colleagues, everything."

That was what must hurt Jeffries as much as anything else, Callie realised. Miller was no longer interested in him.

"He's just having a midlife crisis, if you like." Callie was beginning to feel like a therapist. "He'll snap out of it."

"But meanwhile, this case, I mean…" He trailed off, unsure what to say next.

Callie leant forward and poured them both some more tea.

"So, tell me about the case. Where are you at, what are the Met doing about it?" She looked him in the eye. "Tell me everything."

And after only a very short fight with his conscience, he did.

Danielle Truman had been twenty-seven years old, single, a graphic designer, and had lived near Kings Cross in a rented studio apartment, or bedsit as Jeffries called it. She did not have a regular boyfriend, in fact her colleagues seemed to have assumed she wasn't interested in men.

"No girlfriend?" Callie asked.

"No. Not that they seem to know about, anyway."

She had booked the fisherman's cottage for two nights and taken time off work to come to the Hastings Film Festival. She was very interested in film, had expressed ideas about perhaps moving in that direction, go on a film course, but then a lot of people did and her colleagues didn't seem to know if it was anything other than just a vague possibility for the future.

"She didn't have friends down here? Someone perhaps she was planning to meet at the festival?"

"Not as far as anyone knows. The Met have handled her work colleagues and neighbours and we've interviewed as many of the people involved in the festival as possible. I suggested we put out an appeal, but−" He shrugged and his frustration was evident.

"What about the scene?"

"Clean as a whistle. Partly because the cleaner-cum-owner had already done the downstairs before she discovered the body."

"Didn't she realise something was wrong when she saw the coat and shoes by the door?"

"People often leave things, apparently. She just made a mental note to let the renter know and post them back to her."

Callie could believe that.

"No sign of a break-in?"

"Nah, she definitely let her killer in, that's why the super's agreed it must be a domestic." He ran his hands through his hair again. It didn't make it look any better.

"DNA on the body?" she asked hopefully, but he shook his head.

"Nada."

"Not even where there was that mark?"

He shook his head.

"And no sign she'd been raped or sexually assaulted."

"Fingerprints?"

"Hundreds. The cleaner wasn't that good, but none in the places you'd expect, like on her, or the door, or light switches, just smears there, suggesting they were wearing gloves, or maybe wiped those places down. It'll take an age to get through all the ones we have collected, from books on the shelves, pictures, cooking stuff and what-have-you, but I'm not hopeful they'll be any use at all. You have to remember this place was regularly let out."

She could feel the despair coming off him in waves, and couldn't think of anything to say that would help.

"What do you want me to do?" she asked him. "Talk to Steve?"

"Nah," he snorted. "I don't think even you can help there, Doc – he's a lost cause. No, I was wondering if you could maybe think of something I could take to the super, something we, or I've, missed that might convince him to take the case back."

Callie sat back in surprise.

"Me?"

"Come on, Doc, we all know how you like to get involved."

"Are you saying I'm nosy, Sergeant? Or interfering?" Callie smiled to take the sting out of her words.

"Well…" He grinned back. "If the cap fits?"

She thought for a moment.

"It's hard to know what I could do to help. Do you have any ideas about where you would want me to start?"

"I thought you might be better than me at getting to know the film festival types, find out if any of them knew her, unofficially, like."

He had a point, a good one. Callie hadn't had anything to do with the recent film festival, but she had been interested. She'd even marked up her free programme, meaning to go to one or two events, but then hadn't found time to go to them. She was sure she knew one or two people who had and she would certainly be able to ask a few questions. What harm could it do?

"Okay. I'll do that and let you know if I find anything," she replied and then there seemed nothing more to say so she saw him out and closed the door.

She sat down and absentmindedly sipped her tepid tea. Now who did she know who might have been to the film festival?

The Sounding

Hastings began to be "their" place. They would rent a place for a weekend, a different one every time. It was far enough away from both their homes and workplaces for them to feel safe from meeting anyone they knew, of being outed. They experimented while they were there, at first with sex in the open air and public places, but even with the added fear of getting caught, it wasn't enough. They tried dogging, but the only time that was exciting was when they beat up a man who tried to join in. They left him in a heap, blood pouring from his newly crooked nose and sporting the mark of her nails on his penis.

Another time, he challenged her to pick up a man in a pub, so she went up to a sad-looking man and offered him a quick shag round the back and then led him out to where her partner was waiting to jump on him. They had no idea how badly he was hurt, but the sex they had over his unconscious, nail-marked body was fantastic. Violence was not just a part of the thrill anymore, it was the main ingredient.

They rented different places, not wanting to get known in any particular area, and had begun making copies of the keys. In the first instance, it was to save money, checking with the booking company when the lets were empty and using them without the owner knowing, but when they once again needed to up the ante, do something more to keep the same level of thrill, that's when the idea came to them. It was a flash of brilliance. A way for them to get the ultimate thrill. If violence made the sex so much more than just simple fornication, killing someone would make it even better. It would become a game of life and death.

Chapter 7

"You don't have to be Sherlock Holmes to realise this wasn't a domestic," Callie complained to Kate later.

"No, well, I know you don't want to hear this, but it might be. She seems to have been a private person and unlikely to have picked up anyone while down here, from what you've heard. Perhaps she had a violent boyfriend or a stalker and just didn't tell anyone about it."

Kate had seen far too many domestic violence cases to rule it out so easily, but Callie still wasn't convinced.

They were in the front bar of The Stag, in their favourite seats, close enough to the fire to feel the warmth but far enough away that they didn't feel like they were being baked. There were only a couple of other people in there, all regulars, standing at the bar, but they knew it would get busier later on when the music started.

"Surely, it's more likely that she came down to Hastings with someone. I mean, why would she have come alone?" Kate persisted, as she took another handful of crisps from the packet she had dutifully opened wide so that they could share, even though Callie rarely ate any of them.

"For the film festival apparently."

Kate gave that some thought.

"That does make more sense, then. I can see someone coming down for that on their own."

"Did you go to any of it?"

"I did," Kate replied. "One of the screening events at the Electric Palace. It was for new independent film-makers and the standard was terrific, I think." She didn't sound too sure.

"You think? Distracted, were you?"

"Just a bit, and I'm no expert anyway."

"Who was the distraction?"

Callie knew Kate too well.

"I went with Jenna from the CPS but there was this bloke there, he was just divine to look at and then, right near the end, he opened his mouth to ask a question and his voice! Put me right off."

"I don't suppose you noticed if our victim was there."

"Sorry, I had eyes only for him."

"Diego wasn't with you?"

"Not his sort of thing."

"Doesn't sound like it was yours, either."

"I thought there might be some interesting people there but, to be honest, they were all a bit too earnest for my liking."

Over their second round of drinks, Callie pressed Kate for information about the people she knew who were connected to the festival.

"I really want to get to know more about the victim, Danielle Truman. What events did she go to? Did she buy single tickets? Did she meet up with anyone? You know the sort of thing."

"Surely the police can find all that out?"

"Well, yes, but I'm not sure they are actually looking into it. Not officially anyway."

Kate gave her friend a shrewd look.

"Please don't tell me you are going to look into it unofficially? You will seriously piss off your handsome DI."

"I don't think he'd look up from his phone long enough to notice, if I'm honest."

"He's in love."

"Lust, more like."

"Same difference."

"You can't mean that." Callie was shocked.

Kate hesitated.

"I think for some people, it's pretty much the same."

Callie thought about it, and had to acknowledge that it might be for some people, even if it definitely wasn't for her.

"Well, whatever the reason, he's not paying much attention to the case, and so, Bob Jeffries and I—"

"You have got to be kidding me! You and Bob? That's an unholy alliance if ever there was one!"

Callie waited for Kate to stop laughing before replying.

"He came to see me. He was really upset."

"He must have been if he came to see you."

"Exactly. He is sure that there is a Hastings connection, apart from the fact that the crime actually occurred here, and he feels that it should be properly investigated, not just left to the Met, who seem to be getting precisely nowhere anyway."

"So, what does he think you can do to help?"

"Find out what she did whilst she was down here. That's why I want to talk to the organisers. He's tried, in his own time, but there's a limit to what he can do without it being obvious he's disobeying orders."

"He's not the type to worry about disobeying orders."

"Oh, I doubt he'd worry about the super but this is Miller we're talking about. If Bob finds anything it's Steve he'll be dropping in the—"

"Shit."

"Quite. He does worry about him, you know, and Jayne isn't happy either, but neither feel they can do anything too obviously against orders."

"So, they've left you to do their dirty work."

"Yes." And they had, Callie knew, but she also knew someone had to do it. Someone had to show Miller that he had a job to do and get him away from his phone and his new girlfriend long enough to do it, and Callie couldn't deny that she might take a morsel of satisfaction from being that person.

* * *

Armed with a number of contacts, some taken from the film festival website and others that Kate had come up with, Callie spent Sunday morning on the telephone tracking down anyone who might be able to help her with information on Danielle Truman. She knew she would come up against data protection issues and was not surprised when her first few enquiries hit a brick wall. Having got precisely nowhere and fast running out of options, it was time to use Kate's contacts and maybe Kate herself.

Over Sunday brunch in their usual café, Callie persuaded Kate to call one of the festival organisers. With a sigh, Kate picked up her phone to call someone and, after a bit of a preamble, asked them for information.

"I know, I know, but rules are for the guidance of wise men and the obedience of fools, as they say, and no one could ever call you a fool, Dominic." Kate rolled her eyes to let Callie know what she really thought. "Mmhmm, mmhmm, exactly. I would appreciate you trying … Sure, yes, I'd love to, you know I would … Yes, yes of course … Tonight? … Okay. It's a date."

Callie was leaning forward, desperately trying to hear the other end of the conversation, but Kate leant back; there was no way she was going to let her friend know what she was having to agree to in order to get the information.

"You can log in from home, you say?"

Callie took a sip of Earl Grey tea and relaxed; it looked as if she was going to get the information she wanted.

"That's right – Danielle Truman." Kate continued speaking into the phone for a while longer before finally terminating the call.

"Well?" Callie asked, eager for the information.

"I have to go with him to see a Polish film about people living in sewers," Kate told her.

"You'll love it," Callie replied dismissively. "What about Danielle?"

"I'll hate every moment," Kate was not going to let her off that lightly. "But you will be pleased to hear that Ms Truman only bought single tickets to all the events she attended, and Dominic remembers seeing her at a couple of things on her own. He thinks she must have been gay, by which I mean, I think he hit on her and she rebuffed him."

"That's a lot more than he told the police."

"I'm not surprised he held that bit back. He wouldn't want them to think he tried it on and failed; I mean, they could jump from that little nugget of information to suspecting him of following her home and killing her, couldn't they?"

"And they'd have a point. Do you think–?"

"Dominic?" Kate shrugged. "I can't see it, quite honestly. He's narcissistic enough to take rejection badly, but only to the extent of assuming she didn't like men. Any men."

"Still…" Callie mentally added Dominic to her list of suspects. "Just take care how you handle him when you go on your date."

"Don't worry, I'll let him down lightly." A mischievous smile played on her lips. "Of course, if it puts your mind at rest, you could always come too."

"They will probably have sold out by now," she replied.

But no such luck. There were plenty of tickets available, apparently.

* * *

Jeffries didn't sound pleased when Callie called him and relayed the news that the victim had attended all the events solo, in fact he seemed even more depressed than before.

"It would have been nice if we could positively put her with someone on the night she was killed," he replied.

She hadn't told Jeffries about Dominic trying to chat Danielle up, and failing, because that would inevitably result in him being questioned by the police and the film buff would know Kate had to be the source of their information. She was going to wait until they had been to see the film before saying anything about him. At least it would give her the chance to size Dominic up.

The Circle

It had been so easy, too easy, getting into the house and hiding, and the anticipation as they waited in the smaller of the two bedrooms was almost overwhelming. Almost. It was a shame there had been absolutely nowhere to hide in the main bedroom, but they were nothing if not adaptable. They would manage.

At last they heard the door open and the downstairs lights went on. They stayed silent as they heard her making herself a drink and then the sound of footsteps coming up the stairs. At the top, they both held their breath lest she hear them and come into the room, but there was no problem; she went straight into the main bedroom and switched on the light. It was their cue, their moment to come out of hiding and confront her.

She looked up in surprise as they rushed into the room, covered head to toe in white coveralls, gloves, masks and protective glasses. A terrible sight, frightening, and she couldn't work out where they had come from.

"Wha−!" she started to say before he grabbed her by the throat and pushed her onto the bed. She bucked and fought, kicking out, her feet finding him more than once, but doing little damage with her soft trainers. She tried to grab his hands and when she found she couldn't pull them from her neck, she tore at his coveralls and mask, tearing them. She tried to scratch his face, but he pulled his head back, beyond her reach, and his partner joined in, holding the victim's hands out of the way. All the time he held on to her throat, grunting with the effort. He was too strong, together they were too much, and eventually, she lay quiet. Still and very, very dead.

The woman leant forward and pressed her fingernail hard into their victim's breast twice, leaving two marks, one opposite the other, forming a circle.

Only when she had done that did the man turn, breathless with excitement as he pulled down their masks and kissed his accomplice. There could be no holding back, he had to relieve the built-up pressure. He pulled down his zip and freed his engorged penis. She quickly took him in her mouth, rubbing herself as she did so. He thrust deep into her, gasping in need, and climaxed almost immediately. He pulled back and they both took a moment to catch their breath, before adjusting their clothing.

"That was the so good," she whispered.

But he knew from how she said it that it hadn't been as good as the first time they killed. It had been too easy, too safe. They needed to do something different to keep the levels of excitement high and get the adrenaline rush that they craved. They needed to plan something bigger, better. He could see it in her eyes.

Chapter 8

Callie yawned and looked hard at her coffee mug as if that alone could make it magically refill itself. She was in the doctors' office having finished her morning surgery, and was facing a huge pile of paperwork and wondering how she was going to stay awake long enough to finish it all.

"Late night?" Linda enquired.

"Opposite," Callie told her. "Went to see this film at the Electric Palace. Arty, Polish, subtitled. Slept through it from start to finish and then couldn't get to sleep when I did go to bed."

"Why on earth would you go and see something like that?" Linda laughed as she left, and it was a very good question.

Callie was just finishing her paperwork and trying to stop herself from yawning, when her phone rang. She saw that the number was withheld, which usually meant a call from either the hospital or the police station.

"Hello? Dr Hughes speaking." She listened for a moment. "Oh, hello, Sergeant, just a moment." She stood up to leave the room and there was a collective groan around the table as her colleagues anticipated that she was being called out by the police and would not be doing any visits. Again. And they were right.

* * *

Despite the slight drizzle that had started during the morning, Callie elected to walk to the location she had been given. It would be quicker than going home to pick up her car and she knew that parking would be scarce up on the West Hill. She found the house easily, helped as usual by the proximity of a police car and the uniformed constable on guard outside the property. It was a small post-war house that had been built in the tiny corner space left where two Victorian terraces met at right angles. The wedge-shaped building looked quite big from the front, but Callie could see that it got progressively smaller to the back. The front yard that probably served as the only garden was neat and tidy, but facing north and deeply shaded as well as damp. Moss on the lower parts of the front wall and the doorstep suggested it never really dried out.

As Callie approached the house, the crime scene van pulled up beside it. Colin Brewer, the crime scene manager, leant across.

"Anywhere to park around here?" he asked.

"I saw a couple of spaces up on Priory Road," she replied, knowing that the chances of them still being there were slight.

Brewer grimaced and Callie understood why. Although the street was only a hundred yards or so away in distance, Priory Road was a steep climb from here. Fine for coming down to the crime scene, much harder to lug all the equipment back up.

"We'll just have to block the road for a minute," he said and turned off the engine.

Ignoring the curtain-twitchers and a small group of interested passers-by that was getting bigger by the minute, Callie put her own crime scene bag down at the door and started to put on her coveralls, mask, gloves and shoe covers, whilst Brewer and the driver unloaded some equipment and placed it by the front door. Once Callie was ready, the constable at the door let her into the house.

"Cleaner found her," he said. "In the main bedroom."

It sounded just like the last one, but she needed to keep an open mind.

Inside there was a surprisingly large open-plan living space leading to a small kitchen and, at the back of the room, a steep staircase.

She went carefully up the stairs, although the coarse sisal carpet was unlikely to be a good source of footprints. At the top of the stairs, she could see a shower room to her right, and two open doors to her left. One led to a small room, just big enough for a single bed and a small dressing table; from the door, she could see it was unoccupied. Callie went through the second door that opened into a larger, double bedroom. It was triangular, with the bed jutting out at an odd angle from the longest wall. On the bed, the body of a young woman lay spread-eagled across the pretty blue and white check covers.

The woman was fully dressed, and the bruising around her neck and her suffused face told Callie that, like the first victim, she had been strangled. She noted that the neck of the victim's T-shirt was stretched, and using a gloved hand she pulled it down a little. There, on the woman's left breast was a small circular mark formed by two semi-circles opposite each other. She frowned. She had no idea what these marks signified, but once again, she photographed them and made a note.

Callie then checked for a radial pulse and listened for breath sounds before making a note of the time she was pronouncing death. Formalities over, she looked around the room. There was a chair in one corner and a hanging rail in the other. There was only one shirt on the rail. The overhead light was on, but not currently necessary as there was a large window to let in light. It had bright blue and white curtains to match the bedding, but they had not been drawn.

Callie walked over to the window and looked out. The houses opposite and anyone walking along the street would have been able to see some of what was happening once the light was switched on, if they had been looking.

"Cavalry's here. Pulling up as we speak." Brewer was puffing slightly from the exertion of coming up the steep stairs, placing step plates as he did so.

Sure enough, as Callie looked out of the window, she saw Miller and Jeffries getting out of a silver Mondeo while another marked police car slowly crawled along the street, looking for a parking space. This time, Miller wasn't preoccupied with his phone as he walked towards the house. He looked anxious and Callie understood why. There would be no chance of palming off this case on to another force, not now there were two bodies.

Knowing that Brewer was not going to let anyone else into the house until his team had at least covered the basics and he had set up a more secure pathway, Callie returned downstairs and went out to meet the policemen.

"Watcha, Doc." Jeffries was unable to hide just how pleased he was with the situation, even though it meant that another young woman had died.

"Sergeant," she replied briefly before turning to Miller. "Main bedroom. Single female, fully clothed, looks to have been strangled." She refrained from saying 'just like the last one', with some difficulty.

He just nodded.

"Recent?" queried Jeffries.

"Looks to have been within the last twenty-four hours. Rigor was present but not fully set. So, another weekend killing. Oh, and there's a mark on her left breast again."

"The same?" Jeffries asked.

"Similar, but not exactly."

They didn't seem to know what to make of it either.

"And found by the cleaner again, as I understand it." Jeffries was still smiling as he turned to the constable at the door. "Is she around?" he asked.

"She's in the car, Sarge." The constable nodded towards the marked police car parked further up the road. "English isn't her first language," he added tactfully as Miller and Jeffries turned and walked up the road to interview the poor cleaner.

"Must have been a shock for her," Callie said.

"I should say so," he agreed and then looked relieved as he saw a uniformed sergeant and another constable arrive, armed with clipboards, tape, rubbish bags and signage to secure the scene. "Thank goodness my relief's here, I could do with a break and a coffee."

He did look a bit cold and damp. Callie shivered, she could do with a hot coffee too, and some lunch. She took off her protective clothing and, after a last check that there was no sign of Jeffries or Miller returning, she put up her umbrella, and headed back towards the Old Town.

Chapter 9

Knowing that her afternoon visits would have already been re-booked or taken over by her colleagues, Callie had quickly walked to her home and picked up her car. The café by the police station canteen would not be her first choice if food was the only criteria, but now that she knew it was popular with the detectives there was always the chance of bumping into someone she knew; someone who might have more information about the investigation. Like Detective Sergeant Jayne Hales. And she was in luck; Jayne came in shortly after she got there.

"Stocking up – it's going to be a long afternoon," she explained as she handed over a list of her requirements to the man behind the counter and came over to sit with Callie.

"Do you have any details about the victim yet?" Callie asked as she took a bite of her toasted sandwich and wiped her lips to catch any dribbles of melted cheese.

"Leona Smith, twenty-eight according to her driving licence. She wasn't local. The house is used for short-term and holiday lets. We're tracking down her booking details."

"Strange time of year to be coming to Hastings on holiday," Callie said. "The film festival ended last weekend."

"Yeah, we'll be looking into why she was here once we've done the notification and got someone to do the formal identification."

Jayne's stomach rumbled and Callie cut the end of her sandwich off and offered it to her.

"Are you sure?" Jayne asked politely before taking a large bite out of the hot sandwich in case Callie changed her mind.

"There's no question of this being given to another force, is there?"

Jayne shook her head and swallowed before answering.

"Not a chance. Even if she's from London, the fact that both of them were killed here means we are going to have to take the lead. Speaking of which" – the café owner was waving a cardboard box of sandwiches and drinks at Jayne – "I better get this lot back and finish setting up the incident room. I'll give you a call if there's anything new."

* * *

"She rang me later," Callie told Billy on the phone that evening. "The victim was from Guildford and was staying the weekend in Hastings to visit her grandmother who is in a care home down here."

"Definitely not an investigation that can be handed over to the Met then."

"No, thank goodness."

"I bet Bob Jeffries was happy."

"Like the cat that got the cream."

"So why were these people killed? Do they think someone is targeting visitors?"

"Possibly. Jayne said they were looking into local groups that are anti-incomers, the ones that are always going on about people moving down here."

"I know who you mean," Billy said. "Now what do they call themselves?"

"The anti-FILTH Brigade," she answered. "FILTH as in Failed-In-London-Try-Hastings."

"That's right. Bunch of tossers."

She laughed. "You are only saying that because you are from London."

"But not a failure."

"No. Anyway, I can't believe they would do something like this just to put off incomers. If it is about that, I would have thought the people who are always protesting about second-home owners are more likely."

"Because it pushes prices up?"

"And reduces the number of available properties," she said.

"Seems a little extreme to kill visitors down for the weekend, even if you have been priced out of the house market by people buying second homes."

"I know it does, and the first victim was in a holiday let that wasn't even a second home, it was the owner's only home. She had to move in with her mother whenever she rented it out."

"They might not have known that though," he said.

"You'd think if you felt passionately enough to kill for a cause you'd at least take the trouble to research it properly."

Not that Callie believed in anything to the point where she might kill for it, but she knew that some people did.

Billy seemed to agree. "It doesn't seem like a concrete motive to me, anyway. Although, I bet a couple of unsolved murders has meant house prices have dropped."

"Probably." Callie thought about it. "But knowing how strange and ghoulish people are, it might even put them up."

"That's sick."

"Tell me about it. The other odd thing is that there was no sign of a break-in in either case, meaning the victims must have let their killer inside the property."

"That is strange. You will make sure you don't let anyone in the flat, won't you?"

"As if," she replied, but they both knew she had done exactly that in the past, although she didn't have much choice as her visitor had had a knife. There was a pause in the conversation as they thought about it before Billy tactfully changed the subject.

"So, your trip over here, next weekend?"

"Yes?"

"I've found a country pub that does B&B, not too far from the Giant's Causeway, and booked the night. It's not in a town or anything so it will be just us, away from everyone. Unless you'd prefer to be in a town? The nearest is a place called Bushmills."

"No, the country pub will be fine and you are very romantic, Dr Iqbal." Callie smiled to herself. "I don't suppose your suggestion of staying in this Bushmills place would have anything to do with the local whiskey distillery, would it?"

"Of course not. I didn't know there was a distillery there. What a coincidence."

She could hear the smile in Billy's voice as well, and she was still smiling when the call was long over and she was getting ready for bed. He really was a lovely man. It was just a shame he wasn't currently in Hastings.

* * *

Over the next few days, the papers and local news reports were full of the second murder, with a lot of opinion pieces about someone targeting tourists. Callie shook her head in dismay; that sort of conjecture wouldn't help the town at all. She preferred the reports with a more reassuring tone, mindful that the town depended on tourists, saying that it couldn't possibly be anything to do with visitors and that it was still a perfectly safe place to come and stay despite all the evidence to the contrary.

There had even been an editorial in one of the national broadsheets about people indulging in risky behaviour when away from home, doing things they would never dream of doing in their own backyards, so to speak, and referencing the murders. It made Callie very angry because there was absolutely no evidence to support the view that either woman had done any such thing.

"That's right, blame the victims," Callie muttered.

"Thank goodness the season's over, or as good as over," Linda was saying. "Can you imagine the panic if this happened in the middle of summer. The impact on the tourism industry would be just awful. Let's hope they find the person and get it sorted quickly. Before the spring, at least. It will kill the town otherwise."

And she had a point.

Despite no longer being involved, Callie had watched the news closely, and followed all the press conferences. Miller was looking progressively more haggard. She had to assume the investigation was not going well. One of the local reporters had even got hold of a story about Hastings trying to pass the first murder investigation on to the Met, and Callie was sure that can't have gone down well. She wondered if the source of the story was Jeffries, but couldn't honestly imagine him doing anything so destructive to his boss's career. No, it could have been anyone from the station, and there were bound to be plenty of people who felt they had a score to settle with Miller and who would be only too happy to take him down a peg or two. People he had been promoted above, people he hadn't taken with him, people who felt they should be in his position. He must be having to defend himself on all sides.

"Why don't you go on over and find out what the police are up to," Linda suggested. "It would be good to know they are at least doing something and not just running around in ever-decreasing circles."

And that sense of frustration that Linda was expressing, of a lack of progress, was there in every report and vox-pop interview. The people of Hastings wanted results and they wanted them now.

* * *

The atmosphere in the incident room was very different from the last time Callie had visited the station. There was a feeling of purpose, a busyness to it. There were far more people for a start, and more desks, crammed into the room. Whiteboards at the front were covered with photographs of the victims and the scenes, and there were neatly printed lists of names and notes on lines of enquiry being followed next to them. There was a background murmur of people talking into telephones, finding out about the victims' lives and speaking to the people who called in tips or concerns, or just rang to give the police the benefit of their unqualified opinion.

"Hi Callie." Jayne looked up from her desk and the sheets of information she was going through. "How can I help? Or have you managed to ferret out something that will help us?" She looked hopeful.

"I wish. I'm just calling round to see how things are going. How about here? Anything new?"

Jayne shook her head, sad to have nothing positive to report.

"The boss is in if you want to see him." She nodded towards Miller's office.

Callie glanced over and was taken aback. He looked dreadful, much worse than the last time she had seen him on the news. His face looked drawn, the bags under his eyes were clearly visible and he had lost weight. The case was clearly taking its toll.

Callie went over to his tiny office, knocked on the door and went in. Despite the fact that he appeared to be doing nothing more than stare into space, he looked irritated at her interruption.

"Hi, how's it going?" she asked brightly.

"It's not. Nothing but dead ends," he answered grumpily.

"You used to say that even dead ends were helpful. Trace, interview, eliminate, isn't that what TIE stands for?"

Miller just grunted in reply. If he was pleased to have his own words quoted back at him, he was hiding it well.

His mobile phone began to vibrate on the desk in front of him. He grabbed it and checked the screen, pressing to answer at the same time as saying, "Got to take this, sorry."

He looked pointedly at Callie and then at the door. Taking the rather obvious hint, she turned and went to leave.

"Hiya, darlin'," he said brightly into the phone, just as she was going out.

She tried her best not to slam the door behind her, but somehow, it seemed to do it of its own accord anyway. She flushed slightly with embarrassment as she realised the entire population of the incident room was looking at her, and they all seemed to know exactly why she wasn't happy. She could feel the heat slowly rising up her neck; any moment now and she would have a full-on blush going. She hurried towards the door to the corridor.

"Just a sec, Doc," Bob Jeffries said, pulling on his jacket as he followed her out. "Got time for a cuppa?"

They ended up back at the café down the road; it was beginning to become familiar territory. Jeffries had ordered what he, apparently joking, referred to as 'the heart attack special' and Callie went for an omelette. She had caused a certain amount of confusion when she asked for salad to accompany her meal, rather than chips, but once the owner-chef understood she really did want salad instead of chips, he had complied without too much of a fuss. After all, the customer is always right, even if they are probably in the wrong café.

Callie was careful not to show any reaction as she watched Jeffries put two heaped spoons of sugar in his tea before stirring it vigorously. Looking at the heavily laden plate of fried food in front of him, she could understand why he had referred to it in that way; there must have been enough calories on there to keep a family of four going for a week. It was obscenely excessive even if it did look a whole lot more appetising than her own lunch.

"He looks haggard," she began, once they had both made a start on their food.

"Yeah."

"Has he lost weight?"

"Yeah, all that rabbit food she keeps feeding him." He glanced at her salad in disgust. "Says she likes her men slim, apparently." He forked an enormous amount of runny egg, bacon and hash brown into his mouth and gave it a cursory chew before swallowing and continuing. "Trouble is, it makes him look old and she won't like that, either."

Callie had to agree. The weight loss did make him look older, and not as good-looking. It wasn't as if he had been overweight before; he had just needed to tone up a bit now that he no longer played rugby.

"Maybe I should have a word."

Jeffries snorted into his mug of tea.

"Don't think it would be a good idea to poke your nose in, Doc. He'd likely bite your head off."

She knew he was right.

"And what about the investigation?"

"Making slow progress," Jeffries replied cautiously, then chucked his knife and fork down on the plate in disgust. "Who am I kidding? We're not really getting anywhere, if I'm honest. Don't suppose you've got any ideas have you, Doc?"

Things must really be bad if everyone was asking her for ideas. Unfortunately, she didn't really have any.

"CCTV?"

"We've been through footage from every camera in the vicinity of either crime, and those doorbell ones, where we could get hold of them. No one acting suspiciously on any of them, and no people in common as far as we can tell although it's hard because there's still some bods wearing masks around, you know, because of Covid, and what with it being night time and the poor quality of some of the recordings, it's not that easy to be certain."

"House-to-house?" she asked. "The curtains were open at the second location."

"Yes, but no one saw anything. The people directly opposite were out and didn't get back home until two in the morning. They seem to remember the light being on in the bedroom and the curtains open, but they didn't see anything."

"She was probably dead by then and the killer long gone."

"Exactly."

"I take it there was no significant forensic evidence at either scene?"

"Nothing of interest at all."

"So that tells you this is someone who is very forensically aware."

"That's pretty much everybody these days," he answered morosely. "What with all the stuff about it on television."

"I know, but they usually make mistakes somewhere along the line, get overexcited and forget themselves for a moment. It will happen eventually."

"But that's the other thing, Doc, there's no evidence of anything sexual. No assault, no semen, no pubic hairs, nothing useful at all. So these killings can't be sexually motivated, can they?"

Callie thought for a moment.

"I disagree. Even if the killer doesn't do it there, he gets off on them somewhere, maybe he records it all and watches the films later, or just reruns it in his memories. Believe me, with deaths like these, there has to be a sexual motive in there somewhere, I'm sure."

He didn't look entirely convinced.

"If he's just thinking about it later, he'll need to keep doing it to refresh those memories," Jeffries finally said.

"Yes, I know no one wants to hear this, but I'm sure there will be more if you don't catch him first. Do you have any clues on how he picks his victims?"

"None at all, apart from that they were both staying in holiday lets. Jayne has gone through all their contacts on their phones and email lists and can't find any link between the two women and no mention of meeting people here."

Callie thought for a moment.

"How did they book their stays?"

"Through a website. Well, two different websites, so that can't be the link."

"The killer has to have a way of picking them somehow."

"Not to mention a way of persuading them to let him in." Jeffries stared morosely at his plate. "There just doesn't seem to be anything connecting the two of them."

It wasn't until later that night, lying in bed and failing to sleep, that Callie, still thinking about how the killer picked his victims, had an idea.

Chapter 10

"Hi Jayne, it's Callie here."

Callie was speaking into her mobile phone as she walked across the country park the next morning on her way to work. It was quite cold and she was walking briskly.

"Morning. How's things?" Jayne replied.

"Fine, thanks. Had a few problems sleeping last night."

"Me too. This case is really getting to me. Why did you lie awake?"

"Same reason. Well, in particular, I was thinking about how the killer got into the houses."

"There was no sign of a break-in, in either case."

"I know, but what if he had a key? Or knew the keycode number?"

"Keycode?"

"I noticed the first cottage had one of those key lockboxes on the door, so that the person staying there could just be given the code to the box and there's no handing over of keys. Saves the owner from having to actually meet the people renting their properties. What about the second?"

"Let me check." There were a few seconds silence as Jayne looked through the system. "Yes, the key box is inside the gas meter box on the front of the house." She sounded momentarily excited and then deflated again. "Oh, but there's a note here that says the owners change the code between each letting."

"And the first one?" Callie was disappointed, she had been so sure.

Silence again as Jayne checked more notes.

"She said the same, but she was less certain about the between every client bit."

Callie had reached the stairs at the top of the cliff and stopped looking along the shoreline to St Leonards. Even on a damp autumn morning it was a magnificent view. A thought occurred to her.

"But even if the code was changed, there's nothing to stop the killer copying the key whilst he stays at the place, is there?"

"You think the killer might have actually rented these places before?"

"Well, it would explain how he was able to gain entry, wouldn't it?"

"Bloody hell, it would, but they're not going to like that idea. Do you have any idea how many holiday lets there are in town?"

"I know, it's going to be a lot of work on a long shot—"

"It's not the work that's the problem. It's all the complaints we get when the owners realise the only safe thing to do is change the locks after every letting, or use key card systems like they do in hotels, it would bankrupt some of them."

Callie had to concede that she had a point.

"Maybe they should be doing that."

"It seems a bit much, I mean, I don't suppose anyone could anticipate a killer abusing the system in the way you're suggesting."

"No, thankfully, there aren't too many of those about. At least, I hope there aren't, but it might explain how he got into the properties, if he wasn't invited in, if you see what I mean."

"Yes, and it does at least give us a possible way forward. We need to check everyone who has ever stayed at either place. Right. The guv has just come in so I'll have a word. Bye! Oh, and thanks!"

Callie was glad she sounded enthusiastic again. Any work, any potential lead was probably better than desperately scratching round for some way of moving the investigation forward.

Satisfied to have done her bit, at least for now, and crossing her fingers that something would come of it, Callie headed down the steep steps towards the surgery.

* * *

Callie was dismayed when she looked at her visit list and saw that she was down to see Mrs Conway at Glenalmond again after another apparent fall.

"I can't understand it," Carol, the matron, said as Callie followed her up the sweeping staircase. "I told the girls to keep a close eye on her at night and she has seemed fine during the day."

"Sometimes oxygen levels can drop a little overnight, while you are asleep, and that might be enough to cause confusion."

They arrived at Mrs Conway's door and Carol knocked perfunctorily before entering.

"Hello, Barbie, Dr Hughes is here to see you again."

Callie was pretty sure she hadn't imagined it when she thought she saw Mrs Conway wince when Carol referred to her as Barbie, but the matron seemed oblivious. Mrs Conway was lying on top of the bed this time, with the cot sides raised to prevent her from getting up. She was still wearing the sling from her earlier broken collarbone but otherwise there were no obvious signs of injury. Her beaker of water, TV remote and box of tissues were within easy reach on the bedside table, and a call button was lying beside her hand should she need anything else. Callie came up to the bed and smiled at her patient.

"Hello, Mrs Conway, I hear you've had another fall. Can you tell me if anything hurts?"

"Everything hurts at my age," she replied, but nonetheless still managed a small smile back.

"Let's take a look at the damage then, shall we?"

Callie performed a thorough examination of her patient, checking that the collarbone hadn't been visibly dislodged again and that the ribs were no worse, but found nothing more than some new bruises on the other side of her body. Presumably she had managed to make sure she fell away from her already broken bones.

"Well, it doesn't seem to be so bad this time, but you must call for the nurses if you need anything in the night," Callie told her firmly.

She was surprised to see that Mrs Conway's lips thinned at this and she glanced at the matron, but she didn't say anything.

"You will call the nurses in future, won't you?" Callie persisted, taking her hand and wondering again if perhaps the nurses didn't answer quite as quickly as they should during the night, or even if they might take the call bell away to give themselves a quiet night, but Mrs Conway nodded.

"I promise," she said and gave Callie's hand a little squeeze of reassurance.

Despite that reassurance, Callie spoke to Carol on the way back to the front door.

"How sure are you that the nurses answer the bell promptly at night?"

Far from being affronted at this suggestion, the matron admitted she had been thinking along similar lines.

"I've changed the rota slightly so that the same two people aren't on duty every night just in case. Caused quite a bit of upset doing so, I might add."

Callie could imagine it had. People were bound to settle into comfortable routines and would object to any changes, especially if they thought the changes were in some way a criticism of how well they had been doing their work.

"Well, let's see if that does the trick."

As they came down the stairs, the front door bell rang and Callie could see a figure through the stained-glass window. Before Carol had a chance to reach the door, the bell rang again and there was a knock on the door to go with it.

"Just coming!" Carol called as she hurriedly opened the door to both let Callie out and speak to the person on the other side of it.

The man who had been ringing the bell pushed past Callie and addressed Carol angrily.

"I want to speak to the owners of this care home."

"Mr Conway, I told you this morning your mother is fine, although I'm sure she will be very pleased to see you."

"Fine? Your nurses have let her fall several times now." He turned to Callie. "Are you the person in charge? The owner of this place?"

Before Callie could answer, Carol cut in and, taking his elbow, tried to steer him away from her so that she could leave.

"Dr Hughes is a GP and has just been to check your mother isn't hurt."

He wrenched his arm free and took a step towards Callie.

"You must know what's going on. How did my mother fall this time?"

He was really very close, only a few inches away and speaking directly into her face. It was quite intimidating but Callie stood her ground, just leaning slightly back so that she could at least focus on him, and to stop any spit from landing on her as he spoke.

"Your mother just has a few bruises, this time." She deliberately made her tone very even, trying to diffuse the situation, because he was so angry that he really did seem as if he was about to explode.

"'This time!' Exactly. And last time she had a couple of broken bones, and the time before that, a cut, and the time before that, a banged head!"

Callie tried to hide the surprise on her face as she was completely unaware of the earlier two incidents he was referring to. They were not mentioned in the joint care notes that were kept on all the residents of the home so that visits by different medical and nursing personnel could be logged for everyone to see.

Callie turned to the matron.

"They were very minor falls, we felt we didn't need to involve you," Carol quickly explained to her before she could ask the question.

"I may not be a professional" – Conway glared at Callie – "but even I can see that you can't be looking after her properly here. I want to see her now and I shall be arranging for her to be moved to another home as quickly as possible."

He stormed up the stairs towards his mother's room, with Carol hurrying along behind him.

"Don't do anything rash, Mr Conway, I can assure you that your mother is being well cared for," she said as they disappeared around the corner at the top of the stairs.

Callie had to agree with the man that four falls in a short space of time did suggest a degree of neglect at best and possibly even mistreatment. However, she also knew that moving homes was always disruptive for the elderly and should be avoided if at all possible.

That said, she felt he had good cause for complaint, but it would be far better to get to the root of the problem and improve the care she was receiving at Glenalmond, rather than simply move his mother away. To that end, Callie decided she had to speak to the local commissioning group, expressing her concern and suggesting that they either inspect the home themselves or invite the Care Quality Commission to investigate – not just for Mrs Conway, but for all the other residents as well.

Chapter 11

Jayne flopped down into the seat opposite Callie in Porters wine bar. She looked exhausted and fed up, which didn't bode well.

"What can I get you?" Callie asked after they had exchanged greetings. She had managed to get a table by the window, handily close to the bar.

"A Peroni, please," Jayne replied.

Callie went up to the bar and got the drink, adding it to her tab for the evening, and placed the glass in front of the police officer.

Jayne drank about a third of the beer in one go.

"Bad day?"

"I have spent an entire afternoon going over the lists of people who have rented the two homes. Went back five years, which was actually longer than the second one had been a holiday home. Nada. Not a single name on both lists."

Callie tried to keep the disappointment from her face while she watched as Jayne drank the last of her beer.

"Another?"

Jayne shook her head and picked up her bag.

"Sorry but I've got to get back home."

"Well, thanks for letting me know."

"No problem, it's on my way home. Sorry I don't have better news for you."

Callie was pretty sure the bar was not on Jayne's way home, and she appreciated the detective going out of her way to speak to her, although a beer before facing the family might be essential; it certainly would for Callie, anyway. In fact, she might have been tempted to have another and hope the children were safely asleep by the time she got back.

"At least you looked into it for me."

"Yeah, well, it's one more theory we can scratch off the list. Thanks for the drink, I needed it. Bye."

Callie now had a decision to make. Go home to an empty flat and whatever was in the fridge, pick up a takeaway, or stay and look like some sort of sad loner eating on her own in a wine bar. She glanced up at the menu and was tempted by the posh fish pie, a favourite of hers.

"Been left in the lurch?"

She looked up to see a good-looking man she had never seen before standing beside her table. He had a glass of white wine in one hand and an open bottle of Pinot Grigio, her favourite wine, in the other. "Can I top you up?" He gestured at her almost empty wine glass.

"Er, no thank you, I was just leaving," she said quickly, and grabbing her bag and coat, headed for the door. She had momentarily forgotten that women on their own in bars don't only look like sad loners, they are also assumed to be looking to hook up and the last thing she needed was to be picked up by a stranger.

* * *

"Yes, but he must have been watching me to know what I was drinking." Callie was talking to Kate on the phone, later that evening.

"Could be a coincidence, or maybe just an attentive guy."

"Attentive or creepy?"

"Perhaps you should have hung about to find out."

"No chance. It made me think that if the killer isn't getting into the houses having copied the keys or remembered the code, then perhaps he's picking up these women in bars."

"So now, this bloke is not just a creepy stalker in the bar, he's a serial killer?"

"Well, the killer has got to get into the houses somehow."

"Yes, but men pick up women in bars all the time, and vice versa, I'll have you know."

Callie knew that Kate was much more adventurous in her dating than she could ever be.

"I know, you're right. He was just another lonely man, looking for love."

"Or sex."

"Either way, I'm making too much of it, as usual, but do be careful, won't you?"

"Always," Kate lied. "When are you next seeing Billy?"

They talked about her upcoming trip to Ireland for a while before making plans to meet for a drink in The Stag later in the week and maybe going for a meal in Porters after, so that Callie could finally get her fish pie.

But Callie continued to think about the man in the wine bar. She didn't seriously think he was the killer – after all, it wasn't a weekend – but someone good-looking, charming and with smooth chat-up lines could be targeting lone females in bars, if only to find out where they were staying. Even if the woman didn't invite him back, he could knock on the door later, say she had left something behind, or that he wanted to talk to her and it wouldn't be too hard to persuade someone to let him in, or to push his way in if they refused.

There were lots of bars and restaurants in Hastings where women would feel quite safe going for a drink or even eating on their own. She had been in some of them alone, waiting for someone, or just because she felt like being out rather than staying home. There were places like Porters or The Stag, where she could go for a glass of wine and read a book, or chat to the bar staff and never feel threatened, or strange. As a last resort she could always play with her phone and generally, no one bothered her.

It gave her an idea. Perhaps she could take photos of the two women victims round to some of them; the places where single women might feel they were okay to go for a drink alone, even if they didn't know the area. She thought of brightly lit bars with large, clear windows that meant a woman could check out the clientele before entering, or the restaurants that said they were family or vegan friendly, she thought. Somehow you didn't expect a man out with his family to pounce, or a vegan either, unless it was to try and convert her to veganism. Maybe someone from one of those sorts of places would remember one of the victims coming.

She decided to start with Porters, as she was a regular there, and see if they knew anything about the man who had come over to her table.

* * *

"No, I didn't see him, sorry," Sam, the slight, blonde bar manager said when Callie asked about her mystery man. She called out to one of the bar staff, a muscular young man who was lugging a crate of beer up from the storeroom. "Greg? Did you see a single bloke in here last night, tried to chat up Callie?"

"Nah," Greg said, unhelpfully as he put the crate down behind the bar. "It was busy."

"He bought a bottle of Pinot Grigio about six thirty, maybe a bit later?" Callie prompted.

Greg thought for a few moments and Sam frowned but then went to the till and worked back.

"Here it is, six forty-two, paid cash," Sam said and Greg looked over her shoulder at the till readout. "I don't remember him at all, do you?" she asked Greg.

"Yeah, I do, actually." He looked puzzled. "But he wasn't alone, he had a woman with him. They were both drinking Pinot. Sat over there." He pointed to a corner table, tucked out of the way.

So the choice of drink had been a coincidence. Callie wasn't sure if she was pleased or disappointed he hadn't been watching her all evening.

"He was probably just being kind, thinking you were on your own."

"Maybe." Callie wasn't sure, but it seemed more likely now.

"Or perhaps he was looking for a threesome," Sam said and wiggled her eyebrows at Callie.

Greg looked wistful at the thought.

"Well, he certainly picked the wrong person for that," Callie replied tartly.

"You know if anyone is pestering you when you're in here, you can always come to the bar and tell us," Sam told her. "Greg will deal with them."

Greg nodded, although he didn't look as though he knew exactly what he would do under those circumstances.

"I know, and I would, honestly." Callie fished out some photos of the two victims that she'd printed from the news website. "Did either of these two come in here, do you remember?"

Greg and Sam looked at the pictures.

"I've no idea," Sam said.

"Are they the two girls who got murdered?" Greg asked.

"Yes," Callie said. "They were both in Hastings on their own, and when that bloke tried to chat me up last night, it made me wonder if they met the killer in a bar or something."

"I hope you aren't suggesting one of my customers is a killer, Callie, because that really wouldn't be good for business." Sam was understandably horrified by the thought.

"No, no, I just want to find out where they went, if anyone saw them, that sort of thing." She hastily tried to reassure the bar manager, because she could see that it wouldn't be good, even if the presence of a possible serial killer in the town did mean more press around, and they tended to be good drinkers. She thought it best not say that to Sam, who was back to going through the till receipts as Greg put beer bottles in the fridge. Perhaps she should try somewhere else.

* * *

"Honestly, Kate, I went to every bar, café, and restaurant in the Old Town where a woman might feasibly go on her own, but no one remembered either of the two women being there."

"Sounds fun."

"Not really, they were all anxious to get rid of me, just in case it came out that there was a killer amongst their regulars."

"I can understand that."

"Me too."

"Well he must have met them somewhere."

"Exactly." Callie thought for a moment. "Where would you go?"

"If I was visiting a town for a few days on my own?"

"Yes, I mean, I assumed they would have to go somewhere to eat or drink at some point."

"Not necessarily, that's the beauty of staying in a rented place rather than a B&B, you can cook at home or use takeaways."

"Very true," Callie answered with a sigh. "Maybe I ought to go around all the shops or food places that deliver, see if they recognise the photos."

"Good luck with that." Kate couldn't help laughing at the thought.

Chapter 12

When Callie saw the name Lewis Conway at the end of her morning surgery list, it didn't ring any bells, but then, she didn't know the name of every one of her patients. It was only when she tried to bring up his records on her computer that she found that he wasn't registered at their surgery at all. A brief call to the office upstairs and she understood why he was coming to see her.

"He's the son of one of your patients, um, yes, I've got it, Barbara Conway," Linda told her. "Wanted to discuss her care home and the possibility of moving her." Callie sighed and Linda continued defensively. "I told him it was hard and there was little you could do to help, but he insisted on speaking to you, in person, so I slotted him in at the end."

"Thank you, Linda," Callie muttered sarcastically as she put the phone down and buzzed him in.

"Mr Conway," she said as he came in and even managed to sound happy to see him. "Do sit down. What can I do for you?"

"I need your help, Dr Hughes," he said once he was seated. "I want to move my mother to an alternative home, but everywhere seems to be full, and most even have a waiting list. They said I needed to have proof that my mother's care was negligent in order to be treated as a priority and be moved immediately."

"Well, I don't think I could say that the home was negligent, Mr Conway."

"But you must agree that my mother's care at Glenalmond has been less than satisfactory."

"Well, yes, but—"

"The number of falls she has had, during the night in particular, speaks volumes about the failure of the staff to ensure her safety," he carried on, not giving her a chance to agree or disagree. "There have been four instances that I know about and I have been struck by the complete lack of action by the matron despite my many requests for her to do something to stop it happening again."

"What exactly would you like her to do?" Callie knew that there was a fine line between keeping a patient safe and incarcerating or restraining them. Some families found even the use of cot sides on the bed an intolerable denial of freedom, and there had been lots in the press recently about use of a so-called 'chemical cosh', the use of sedative drugs to ensure that confused elderly patients were quiet at night, or during the day in some cases. To her knowledge, Glenalmond didn't advocate the use of any kind of restraint, other than the use of cot sides to prevent the patient falling out of bed accidentally.

"I put it to the matron that someone should be stationed in my mother's room overnight, but she said it wasn't possible."

"One-to-one care of that sort is very expensive, Mr Conway." Callie tried to placate him. She could well understand the matron refusing to go to that sort of length, unless Mr Conway was prepared to pay for it. "The home will probably only have two carers on duty overnight, and to expect one to stay with your mother would seriously impact on the level of care being given to the other residents."

"I don't care about the other residents!" he exclaimed. "I just want my mother to be safe and she isn't!"

"Of course, of course, and I quite understand that" — Callie tried to soothe him — "but there are limits to what the matron can do, within her budget. Now, what I suggest is—"

"I want her moved, Dr Hughes," he interrupted again. "I want you to write a letter saying that my mother has been neglected."

"I really don't think, in all honesty, I can say that at this stage. I have the other residents to think about — but rest assured I will be working with the home and its staff to try and improve the situation."

"I might have known you'd be on her side!" he shouted and stood up. "None of you will do anything. You don't believe me, but it doesn't matter, I can do it myself, I'll prove they are mistreating her, I will! I've already set it in motion and I'll tell everyone you tried to cover it up, once I have the evidence. Just you wait and see, I'm getting the proof and you will be sorry!"

And, with that, he stormed out of the room, slamming the door behind him. Callie sat there, thinking about what had just happened, trying to work out whether she could have handled it, or more precisely him, better.

There was a knock at the door and Linda poked her head into the room.

"Well, he was a bit upset as he left, what on earth did you say to him?"

"I really don't know," Callie replied but she kept going over the conversation in her mind, particularly the phrase "I've already set it in motion." She picked up the phone. The least she could do was warn the care home that he might have done or be planning to do something rash.

* * *

"Can you do Dr Grantham's Saturday surgery, Callie?" Linda asked when she went up to the office later. "Only something urgent's come up."

"Sorry, I'm away this weekend," Callie replied, with regret. She would normally have been happy to cover for one of her colleagues given the number of times they had to cover for her, but she was going to Belfast to meet up with Billy and there was no way she was going to cancel that.

"I don't often ask," Dr Grantham said, irritably. Callie hadn't seen him come into the room behind her.

"I know, and normally I would do it, of course I would, but—"

"It really is most ungrateful of you," he said before she could explain. "We'll have to get a locum in, which you know I hate to do to our poor patients, making them see someone who knows nothing of them or their history."

"That's always supposing we can get one at such short notice," Linda grumbled.

"I'm really sorry, Hugh, can't one of the others do it?"

"I can't ask any of them, they have families too and they do more than their fair share of extra work because of you." Dr Grantham stalked out of the room, leaving Callie reeling.

"What was that all about?" she asked Linda.

"I don't know but you seem to be upsetting a lot of people today, so why don't you go and take a walk and think about it while I try and find cover for the Saturday morning session."

Linda picked up the phone and Callie decided she was right; a walk would do her good.

* * *

A walk might well have been a good idea, but she had only gone a few yards when the heavens opened. As Callie sheltered in the doorway of the Sea Life Centre, she gave some thought to Linda's words. She couldn't really be the cause of all these people being so angry, could she? She honestly didn't think she could have done anything to prevent Lewis Conway losing his temper with her, apart from promise to write and say the home staff were neglecting his mother, which would have made them even more upset than he was.

However, she did feel guilty about not being able to stand in for Hugh Grantham. He, and her other colleagues, had so often helped her out, but she did her best to make up for that, doing more than her fair share of on-call, nights, weekends and even baby clinics. And what choice did she have? Much as Billy understood about the demands of her work – and his job was as bad if not worse – if she had agreed to stay, moving her Belfast flight from Friday night to Saturday afternoon, he would have been seriously put out. He had made loads of plans for their weekend, hired a car, booked hotels and restaurants. He would have been even more irritated than Dr Grantham if she had changed their plans and, worse, he might think she wasn't trying hard enough to keep their relationship going.

As she stood, watching the rain, she wondered if that were true. Did the fact that she had considered changing her flights, even for a moment, mean she wasn't committed? Or just that she took her work seriously?

She sighed and mentally shrugged. She didn't know the answer, but she had made her decision. On this occasion, Billy had won but she had no idea if he would continue to do so. Only time would tell.

The rain didn't look like stopping so she turned and went into the visitor attraction, pulling the pictures of the two victims from her pocket as she did so. She might as well do something useful whilst she waited for the rain to stop.

Chapter 13

"Are you expecting a round of applause?" Kate asked sarcastically when Callie told her about her decision not to do the Saturday morning surgery. "It's about time you started thinking of yourself."

"I know, but I still feel guilty about it."

Kate didn't deign to reply to that and merely shook her head in mock despair.

"Have you got any further with your search into where the two women might have met their killer?"

"Not really." Callie picked up the mug of tea Kate had made for her and leant back into her wonderfully saggy and battered sofa. She wondered if she should get a new one for herself; the seating in her flat looked very stylish but was nowhere near as comfortable as this. Perhaps some cushions would improve the situation? Not as bright and eclectic as Kate's collection but something to add a little muted colour and soften the image. She sighed contentedly before continuing. "I did find out that Danielle Truman had been to the Sea Life Centre whilst she was here, but no one seemed to recognise the second victim, Leona Smith."

"Going to the Sea Life Centre's not exactly suspicious, is it? I mean, lots of people go there."

"I know, but it's also the only place other than the film events that anyone's recognised her, and Leona doesn't seem to have been anywhere except to visit her grandmother at the care home in Bexhill."

Callie briefly wondered if she should have visited the home and seen whether there was any connection, but she couldn't imagine there would be, and she couldn't really think of a reason to go all that way and ask questions.

"Have you been keeping Jayne Hale up to date with all your enquiries?" Kate teased, "Or DI Miller?"

"I've been talking to Bob Jeffries, actually." Callie could feel her neck redden as she admitted this and Kate roared with laughter.

"I don't believe it! You and Bob Jeffries, still having secret meetings? Plotting behind his boss's back? The gossips would have an absolute field day!"

"Nothing untoward is happening."

"Don't worry, I believe you, but that doesn't mean to say everyone would."

"Go on with you, there's no way anyone at all would believe there was anything going on between us. I mean, Bob Jeffries? Are you serious?"

Callie laughed but knew she was wrong to be so certain; there was always someone who would believe even the most blatantly outrageous gossip. Bob Jeffries might survive the rumours, he might even revel in the notoriety, but she wouldn't. She would never be able to show her face at the police station again if anyone suggested she and Bob were having an affair. She might even have to move away. Go to Belfast. But if she did follow Billy, she wanted it to be a free choice, not forced on her in a way that made her resent it, and perhaps resent him. She would have to be very careful in future. Very careful indeed.

* * *

Callie hurried through her evening surgery, hoping to finish as quickly as possible so that she could get to the airport in good time for her Belfast flight. She had done extra visits during the afternoon and made sure all her paperwork was up to date before starting her evening list but the atmosphere in the office was still frosty. One of her colleagues had agreed to do the Saturday morning surgery for Dr Grantham as no locum had been available at such short notice, and they all wanted her to feel guilty about this. She did, up to a point, but not so guilty that she was going to cancel her weekend away with Billy. She was really looking forward to seeing him. In fact, the amount she had missed him and wanted to see him made her wonder again about her future. Was it here? Or there?

Last patient seen and final prescription signed, Callie almost ran down the stairs and out to her car, trying to ignore the persistent ring of her phone. A quick glance told her it was the matron at Glenalmond. If it had been an urgent problem, the matron would have called the surgery or dialled 999, so Callie let it ring out and go to voicemail. She was sure she would have time to listen to the message once she was checked in and waiting for her flight to be called, but traffic jams and the persistent rain meant she only just got to the airport in time and had to run to get on her flight before the gate was closed. The message had to wait until she got around to listening to it much, much later.

* * *

Billy was waiting for her in the arrivals area when she came through, and he whisked her to where he had left the car and then drove her to the small pub where they were staying near the north coast. It wasn't until the next day that they emerged from the bedroom and ventured downstairs for breakfast. Not having eaten since Friday lunchtime, Callie was ravenous.

Billy ordered the full Ulster fry, but Callie baulked at the vast amount of food the menu listed as included in it and asked for the light breakfast instead.

"You're not a veggie, are you?" the elderly man serving them demanded in a slightly derisive tone.

"No, just not sure I could eat more than that," she said and wasn't sure she had said the right thing.

"You need a full belly at the start of the day if you're to get anything done," he said ominously and disappeared into the kitchen.

"Full belly doesn't even begin to describe how I feel," Callie moaned as she climbed the stairs to their bedroom having eaten far too much. The light breakfast hadn't been all that light and with cereal, juice, and toast, she reckoned she had eaten enough to last her all day. She couldn't understand how Billy had managed to eat all of his, particularly as throughout the meal they had been subjected to a blow-by-blow description of the treatment their elderly server had been made to undergo for his cancer of the appendix after Billy had rashly admitted that they were both doctors. The man had then gone on to ask advice for a number of friends and relatives with strange medical problems their own doctors couldn't diagnose.

"Thank goodness you didn't tell him you were a pathologist, he would have probably got on to all his relatives that had ever had autopsies and the strange things that killed them."

"I thought the other guests were looking quite green enough," he said with a laugh. "Come on, get your walking gear on, we've got lots to do today and we need to work off that breakfast."

With the visit to the Giant's Causeway, walks along the coastal path, visiting the Bushmills distillery and lots of eating, drinking, and laughing, the weekend passed far too quickly and Callie didn't actually listen to her voicemail until after she had arrived back in England. In fact, not until after she had called Kate on the Sunday evening to tell her all about her weekend away Billy.

"He tried really hard, bless him," she told her friend.

"Do you think he's trying to persuade you that you would like Belfast?"

"We didn't actually see much of the city."

"Too busy doing other things, eh? Nudge nudge, wink wink!"

"No, well, yes and no, but we were staying near the coast in a really quirky pub and the food portions were just enormous. I think I must have put on about a stone."

"Sounds like my kind of place."

After some further discussion of her visit, Callie finished the call and only then noticed the voicemail icon on her phone reminding her that she still hadn't listened to the message.

With a sigh, she did.

"Oh dear, um, Dr Hughes?" the matron said in the flustered manner of everyone having to leave a message instead of managing to speak to an actual person. "Mrs Conway had another fall, well two, nothing major, but I called her son and he came at once, saying that he'd be taking action against us now that he had the proof. I don't know what he meant by that. She seems absolutely fine, but I just thought it would be good if you checked her over again, just in case he does take some sort of action. So perhaps you could come and see her over the weekend, or early next week?"

She sounded worried and Callie couldn't blame her. She would get Linda to add the care home to her visit list in the morning. Meanwhile, she had some unpacking to do and she needed to sort out her clothes for the week, but as she did these things, she couldn't help wondering about the matron saying that Lewis Conway had told her that he had proof now and wondering what on earth he could have meant by that.

The Line

In their continual search for something different, something more exciting to add to their sex games, their killing games, they decided that this time, she should be more involved, more hands on, not just a voyeur. That was why they had picked this location.

They knew the owner often came down from London and stayed there himself, and that the owner was a man. Another change-up, another risk added. He was a young man, in his thirties, but he looked slight, and they thought it could work, particularly if the man was drunk, if they made sure he was drunk, or drugged. There were two of them, and they would have the element of surprise.

Meeting their target before the event was risky, but that also added to the excitement. They had mapped out as many CCTV cameras as they could on previous visits, so they knew how to avoid them and which pubs might have them too, so they knew they were pretty safe when he walked towards Hastings and went to one of the bars in a backstreet.

She had chatted to him in the bar he went to. She allowed him to buy her a drink and then she bought him one, adding a few drops of GHB, and then made her excuses as his speech became slurred. She followed him back to his home, keeping close, but she needn't have worried, he was too drunk and drugged to notice her. He was weaving and stumbling, but still able to get himself back to the flat; that had been her main worry, there was no way she would have been able to carry him, and it would have been too risky.

Safe in the knowledge that her partner in crime was already in the man's home, fully suited in protective clothes, she saw their target safely up the stairs and quickly took her own gear out of her large handbag and dressed herself up in it. Her excitement rose as she was getting herself hurriedly ready for what was about to happen, anxious in case anyone came out of their flats and saw her, dressing in the stairway.

Finally ready, she went up the last few steps and into the corridor. There were lots of doors, and she could see him looking confused as he tried to open his, the key was turning but the door wouldn't open and he couldn't work out why. He looked up and checked he had the right door, even looked at the next one along to be sure, before trying to open it again.

"Hello again," she said and knocked on the door, three short raps, a pause and then a fourth. Their agreed code.

He seemed to recognise something about her, but wasn't sure. Could this be the same girl he had talked to earlier? If so, she had changed and it was wrong, very wrong. The last time he saw her she had been in a low-cut top and jeans, she hadn't been in paper coveralls, and her hair hadn't been hidden by a shower cap, her face by a mask. He turned back, surprised as the door suddenly opened. He said, "What the fuck?" but she pushed him into the flat and closed the door gently behind them, before any neighbours came out to see what was up – if there was anyone near enough to hear.

He'd struggled, of course, but there were two of them and he was soon flat on his back on the bed and she was straddling him, tightening the scarf around his neck, pulling as he bucked and kicked and tried to throw her off. He couldn't, of course, because he was being held down by her partner, but he managed to turn onto his stomach which actually made it easier and it wasn't long before the struggling ceased along with his gasps for breath and he lay there, dead. She had done it! To mark her success, she turned him half over and she pressed her nail into his chest three times, making a line across his breast. She let him fall back into the prone position and then turned to her partner, needing him.

She had never felt so alive, so exhilarated as she kissed her lover and sucked him off, all the while rubbing herself to an overwhelming climax.

"That was the best," she whispered, "the best ever."

Chapter 14

Callie was only halfway through her morning surgery when she got the call from the police. If refusing to change her weekend plans had irritated her fellow doctors, leaving them with extra work on a Monday, the busiest day of the week, wouldn't exactly make them happier.

Thankfully, she left Linda to explain why they were having patients added to their surgery and visit lists and hurried to the address she had been given. It was a studio flat in Marine Court, the iconic art deco building on the seafront in St Leonards that had been designed to imitate a cruise ship. Despite its rich history, Callie had never actually been inside the building, not even to visit a patient. She hurried up the stairs and through the corridors until she found the door with a policeman stationed outside.

She hastily donned her protective crime scene clothing before she entered the flat. There was a bathroom to her left, and then the room opened out, with a sleek, modern kitchen area to one side, and chairs and a coffee table in a corner by the window. Once she had taken a few steps into the room, she could see a bed, backing on to the bathroom wall and facing the amazing panorama of the sea. What a beautiful view to wake up to every morning, she thought and then glanced back at the bed.

To all intents and purposes, the scene was remarkably similar to the last two she had attended, with the exception that this time she could see the fully dressed corpse lying face down on the bed was that of a young man. She crouched down to get a closer look at his face, which was turned to one side. It was suffused, blue, with visible petechiae. That, and the deep red mark around his neck, suggested that strangulation was the cause of death.

She felt for a pulse and pronounced him dead. It wasn't hard, he had probably been dead a while, as he was cold to her touch and there was no sign of rigor when she picked up and dropped his arm. She would leave more formal measures to the crime scene techs and the pathologist, but she suspected he had been dead at least a day or possibly two. She couldn't see if there were any marks on his chest given his position, but made a note to ask the pathologist.

"What have we got here?" she heard Colin Brewer ask the policeman outside the door.

"I've just pronounced death," Callie called to him as she walked around the edge of the room, following, as closely as possible, the path she had taken on her way in to the scene.

From the doorway, Brewer closely watched the route she was taking and, leaning forward, placed plastic plates for her to step on, as far as he could reach. Once she was in the corridor, he stepped forward, crossing the room and carefully placing more plates so that any other footprints would not be disturbed. The laminate flooring would be a good surface for collecting them, provided it hadn't already been cleaned.

She turned to the constable at the door.

"Was it a cleaner who found him?" she asked.

"Yeh, she's downstairs with the sarge."

"I can't imagine she did much cleaning before she saw the body," Callie said to Brewer.

"No, thank goodness. One benefit of a studio apartment."

Callie nodded a greeting to several more techs arriving to process the flat as she went downstairs. She found that Sergeant Munroe had persuaded one of the shops on the ground floor to let him use their staff break room and to bring hot, sweet tea for the cleaner. It wasn't much, but it was better than taking her outside in the cold and interviewing her there.

"Hello," Callie said gently, "how are you doing? Must have been a terrible shock for you."

The young woman, dressed for work in jeans and a sweatshirt, sleeves rolled up, nodded weakly and sipped her tea.

"I've never seen anyone, you know, dead before."

"It must have shaken you up a bit."

"I'll say." The woman nodded and gave Callie a tentative smile. "He was all right, was Simon."

"He owned the flat?"

"Yeah, comes down weekends, unless he's let it out, that is. He lets me know when he needs me to come in and clean."

"Watcha, Doc," Jeffries said behind Callie, making her jump.

"Sergeant Jeffries," she acknowledged him.

He jerked his head at the door and went out again. She assumed he wanted her to follow him.

"Just a minute," she said and turned back to the cleaner. "Take care now," she said to the young woman and went out to the small area at the back of the shop where Miller was once more focused on his phone, but at least he looked up when she came out of the room.

"This isn't the same, is it?" he asked. "I mean it's the homeowner and it's a man."

"Yes and no," she said. "You are right that he is a young male, but the cause of death is almost certainly strangulation and he's fully clothed like the other two.

Also, despite being the owner, it's a second home and he lets the place out when he isn't using it."

"Bloody hell," he growled, and even Jeffries looked shocked, although he was guilty of far worse language as a general rule, but neither he nor Callie had ever heard Miller swear before.

"An agency, or does he do private lets? Friends and family sort of thing?" Jeffries asked.

"I don't know. You'll have to ask the cleaner, she seems to know him."

She left them to do their job, but it did set her wondering again. How was the murderer picking his targets, and why?

* * *

Callie had been expecting Dr Grantham to have a little moan about her having been called out and leaving her colleagues with extra work again, but nothing prepared her for the onslaught she got when she came into the office.

"It's just not good enough," he said as soon as she entered the room.

Callie was so surprised that she stood stock still, in the middle of the office, and said nothing. All the admin staff looked up and similarly froze.

"You cannot expect your colleagues to pick up your slack and do your job for you," he continued.

Linda finally got over her surprise and responded by standing up and coming out from behind her desk.

"Perhaps we could take this elsewhere," she said calmly and ushered them both out of the office and away from the staff who were gagging to hear more.

Once out of the office, Linda opened the door to the doctors' room.

"Could you give us a moment?" she told the two GPs in there and Callie could see they were surprised and about to protest, as she would have done in their place.

"Now, please?" Linda said in a voice that made it clear they had no choice, and the sight of Callie and Dr Grantham standing behind her spurred them into action.

Once they were alone in the room, Linda closed the door.

"I'm sorry," Dr Grantham apologised, "I shouldn't have said it in front of everyone, but I mean it, Callie. It's too much. On a Monday as well. You can't flit in and out of a job like this. You need to think about your future. You are either committed or not, and if the answer is not, I think you should go." He turned on his heel and went out.

"What on earth has got into him?" Callie finally managed to say in surprise.

"He's been under a lot of pressure lately." Linda looked as though she would like to say more about that but stopped herself. "And you have to admit, you have been missing a bit more than usual – or rather, a lot more than usual."

"There have been three murders, Linda! And yes, I booked a weekend off so that I could visit Billy, but I wasn't due to work that weekend and he can't expect me to drop everything and do his on-call for him."

"But that's exactly what you expect the others to do."

"You know that's different. It was agreed when I took this post that I would work part-time, and be paid part-time, so that I could also work for the police."

"Well, let's just say that perhaps Dr Grantham's having second thoughts about that."

"It's a bit late now."

"I know, I know." Linda sighed. "Look, Callie, there are things going on that I can't talk about yet, but he's under a lot of pressure, personal pressure." She looked meaningfully at Callie, trying to convey facts that she couldn't actually say. "And perhaps you need to be a bit more understanding, and be more present and supportive for a while."

She went out and the other doctors came back in, looking a bit sheepish.

"Do you know what's going on with Hugh, Gauri?" Callie asked Dr Sinha.

"No, I don't, but maybe you – well, we all – need to give him a bit of space."

"And that doesn't mean swanning off and leaving him to do more work than he already does," added Dr Mackie, the newest partner, leaving Callie in no doubt that she didn't have any support there.

Chapter 15

The matron took a while to respond when Callie finally arrived at Glenalmond, trying to do as many of her visits as possible before evening surgery.

"Come on, come on," she muttered as she waited for the door to open.

"Dr Hughes, thank you so much for coming again," the matron said as she hurriedly let her in.

The older woman puffed and panted as she tried to keep up with Callie's swift pace up the stairs, arriving at Mrs Conway's room some way behind her.

"Oh dear," Mrs Conway said as Callie entered the room. "They really shouldn't have called you out, Doctor. I'm absolutely fine."

"That's as maybe, Mrs Conway," Callie said, "but we really have to get to the bottom of why you keep having these falls."

"I do hope this isn't all because of my son, he means well, but sometimes I think he takes things a bit far."

"I'd be here to check you over, whatever, Mrs Conway. Now can you tell me what happened? Did you get up in the night to go to the bathroom?"

The matron interrupted and scolded her. "You should ring for a bedpan, you know that, Barbie."

Both Callie and Mrs Conway winced.

"I didn't need the lavatory," Mrs Conway said truculently.

"So why did you get up?" Callie asked quickly before she could be interrupted again.

"Well, sometimes I can't sleep, Doctor, and my legs get restless and uncomfortable, you know, with cramp, and I just have to get up and walk a bit to ease them."

"We all get that from time to time, but if it happens a lot, I can give you something that might help."

"I really just need to get up and move."

"We all need to do that from time to time." But most of us don't fall over when we do, Callie didn't add. "And what happens when you fall? Why does it happen? Do you feel faint?"

"Oh, no, it's just silly reasons. I trip on the rug, or my slippers fall off, things like that."

Callie wasn't convinced by this story, there were no rugs in the room and Mrs Conway's slippers were sturdy ones that wouldn't come off easily – always supposing she bothered to put them on.

"You remember falling then?"

"Yes."

"And you didn't feel dizzy?"

"No, dear, I just trip, that's all. Perhaps I need new slippers."

Callie still wasn't convinced.

"The cold floor on your bare feet really helps cramps, doesn't it?"

"Yes, it's such a relief," Mrs Conway agreed.

After she had examined Mrs Conway and confirmed that there were no new injuries, Callie left the room with the matron.

"I saw what you did there," the matron said with a smile. "She can't be tripping on a rug because there aren't any, and it can't be her slippers, because she doesn't put them on."

"Exactly," Callie agreed. "Look, I'm going to add some medication to help with night-time cramps and restless legs, and I'll order a few tests, bloods, ECG and such like, just to see if we can find anything."

And Callie hurried out; she had to get back on time to do her surgery and make sure she didn't upset Dr Grantham any further.

* * *

Callie put a large glass of Pinot Grigio on the table and took off her coat before sitting down. The glass had one cube of ice in it, just the way she liked.

"We must stop meeting like this – people might start to talk," Bob Jeffries said.

This was so similar to the talk she had had with Kate that Callie momentarily wondered if they had spoken to each other, before putting it out of her mind. Kate and Bob weren't friends and didn't even like one another, so they were hardly likely to be communicating behind her back.

Bob had a full pint of beer in front of him, and an empty packet of crisps. A quick glance at her watch told her that she was about half an hour late for their agreed meeting.

"Sorry," she said. "Mammoth surgery."

"That's okay, I like pubs."

Callie looked around her, The Hastings Arms wasn't one of her regular haunts, but she had been there a few times and Jeffries seemed quite at home there. In the summer it tended to be too full of tourists for her liking, but this time of year it was quieter and had more of a local feel. Callie took a sip of her wine; it was very nice too, and just what she needed.

"How's it going?" she asked him and was surprised to see him smile.

"At least the super has agreed to up the budget and set up a proper investigation. Steve is SIO, not that he's happy about it, but even he knows he can't pass the buck this time."

"It's a relief they are taking it seriously." Callie knew that a 'proper investigation', as Jeffries had called it, involved seconding a lot more than just personnel and sourcing extra equipment to run the incident room; it meant allocating a significant part of the police budget to it, as well. The super was unlikely to be happy at that, any more than Miller was likely to be happy with the extra work.

"They had no choice after three bodies," Jeffries said. "Cheers!"

He grinned at her and raised his glass before downing a considerable portion of his beer. It seemed strange to be toasting another death.

"Cheers!" she reluctantly agreed, before turning to why they were meeting. "What's the story with the new victim?"

"Nicholas Bentley. It's a second home for him in a way. He lives in London, rents, but couldn't afford to buy up there, so got himself on the property ladder down here with the idea that he might be able to build up some equity and afford a place nearer his work before he reaches retirement age. He spends quite a few weekends and some holidays in the flat, but he rents it out as much as possible in between to cover the costs."

"He sounds very sensible," she said.

"Not if you listen to the locals who think they have some sort of God-given right to own a house in the town just because their parents did. They can't seem to understand they can't afford one if they don't earn as much as an accountant in London."

"And I can see their point, but at least he brought visitors to the town and tourists bring in money."

"I don't suppose they think that's enough compensation for being priced out of the housing market."

"No," she conceded. "They probably don't. Did he use a company to advertise the flat?"

"Yeah, but a different one to either of the first two locations."

"That's a shame." Bang goes that theory, Callie thought. "What about people who've rented it though? Any names in common?"

"It'll take Jayne and Nigel a while to get through them, but not so far."

He looked out of the window. Callie could see the entrance to a rather more modern bar and restaurant. Not one she had ever frequented, and it seemed packed full of a younger crowd, drinking lager and cocktails and being way too noisy for her. With a start, Callie realised she had aged; at one time that was exactly the sort of place she would have enjoyed. When had she got so old?

"I spoke to the pathologist," she said with a sigh.

"Oh yeah? What about?"

"The marks on the bodies. On their left breasts. He said the man was marked as well, so it definitely looks like the same murderer."

"What are the marks from?"

"They look like nail marks, but no one knows what they signify. The pathologist sent me a photograph." She showed him the picture of the man's chest with a line of three nail marks across his left breast.

"Weird," was all he said, clearly not interested. "How about you?" he asked her and she had to think for a moment before understanding what he was asking.

"The only place I've found that either of the two women visited was the Sea Life Centre," she admitted. "Oh, and the old people's home in Bexhill where the second victim's grandmother lives. But in each case, it was only one of them. I've been round all sorts of places; bars, restaurants, art galleries, but no one recognises them."

"Doesn't seem like they're being picked up anywhere in particular then," Jeffries said morosely. "Although I might still try and persuade the boss to let me go around showing their photos at a few pubs."

Callie could imagine that was just the sort of job he would enjoy.

"Sorry – been there, done that, for the women anyway, and didn't find anywhere," she said. "What about the third victim, the man?"

"We're still trying to find out what his movements were over the weekend. All we know from his work colleagues is that he said he was coming down to Hastings on Friday night and that he came by train. He had to leave dead on time to catch it, they said."

"Partner?"

"No one regular, apparently, but they don't seem to know him that well, and none of them socialised outside of work. Spoke to his next of kin, his parents in Bedford, but they didn't seem to know about any one special in his life."

"Gay?"

"Again, not according to his parents, but we all know that doesn't mean anything."

"And no forensics?"

"Not a thing as yet, but we live in hope." He took another swig of beer. "Oh, but there is a fair amount of CCTV in the streets around Marine Court and out the back. One of the cameras covering the entrance he would have used was broken, but there were others at the back of the shops, so Nigel's going through all that footage. You never know, they might have something."

"And do you think our killer broke the one covering the entrance."

"It'd be a pretty big coincidence if he didn't, but there were no prints or DNA to be found on it," he added before she could ask the question. "So basically, we've got nothing," he said morosely. And Callie had to agree.

Jeffries looked out of the window and tensed. Callie looked out and saw Miller, with a young, blonde woman on his arm. She was wrapped in an expensive-looking coat and with her shiny gold hair, shimmery blusher, and large diamonds at her throat and in her ears, she seemed to almost glow and twinkle as she moved. Miller had his arm round her as he opened the door to the bar opposite them. They were both laughing, engrossed in each other, and Callie couldn't help notice that Miller's hand had slipped down to his girlfriend's bottom as he ushered her through the door in front of him. Callie looked at Jeffries, he was scowling.

"He'd better not be hungover tomorrow," he said, downing the rest of his pint. "Do you want another?"

Callie declined the offer and made her way home, leaving Jeffries to quietly get drunk. If she was a gambler, she would bet that both men would be hungover in the morning.

Chapter 16

Callie spent most of the week trying to keep out of Dr Grantham's way. Whatever was going on with him, she didn't want to be the source of his anger again. She had volunteered for extra visits, and was on call for the whole weekend, hoping to persuade everyone that she was a worthwhile member of the team.

"Is he sick or something?" Kate asked when Callie arrived, belatedly, for their regular weekend brunch and explained why.

"Could be, I've no idea what's going on, but he is definitely not in a good mood. He even suggested I should resign."

"Are you going to?"

"No! Well, not yet, anyway."

"So, you are thinking about it?" Kate sounded worried.

"Well..." Callie gave it some thought as she ate. She would love to be with Billy, of course she would, and she was fairly sure that she would be able to find a job as a GP in Belfast; in fact she'd found a city centre practice that was advertising in the medical press. She was thinking about giving them a call, to see how the land lay, so to speak. What she wasn't so sure about was getting a placement as a forensic physician with the police. Did it work the same way in Belfast? Perhaps she should research it, in case, but would she want to do it there anyway? Northern Ireland had its own problems, of course, but were they so very different from Hastings?

She had broached the subject with Billy but he hadn't noticed any difficulty at all in being accepted. That was probably because he was so obviously not affiliated to one side or the other and neither he, nor his family, would be suspected of any involvement in the previous troubles, she thought. It was the same for Callie, in that she wasn't religious and had no Irish family, but she only had to open her mouth for everyone to know she was English. Would that be a problem? With some people, anyway. She didn't know. All she knew was that it did sometimes matter where you lived in the province as some areas were entrenched in one side or the other so she wanted to try and avoid those, but would it matter to her patients if she was English? Perhaps she needed to speak to someone actually doing the job in Belfast and get a heads-up before she went any further.

"I really don't know if I want to go," she finally admitted to Kate. "I'd have to research it all a bit more, see how it is, and how it might be for me – you know – how I would fit in."

"It sounds like you have certainly been giving it some thought."

And she had been, that was true. The problems at work had definitely made her do so, as well as the fact that she was missing Billy so much. It also hadn't escaped her notice that it was after seeing Miller and his new girlfriend that she had spent the rest of the evening looking at the job advertisements and found this particular one in Belfast. That had nothing to do with her motives though, she told herself sternly; it was because she was unhappy at work and wanted to be with Billy that she was considering it.

Kate tactfully changed the subject. "Have you heard any more about the murders?"

"Well, as you've probably seen on the news, the investigation is firmly back in Hastings."

"Hmm," Kate said, "I saw Steve Miller at one of the press conferences. You are so right about his hair and the weight loss. It really doesn't suit him."

"Did I tell you I saw him with his girlfriend?"

"No! Tell me more. What's she like?"

"Gorgeous. I can quite understand why he's smitten. It's Bob Jeffries I feel sorry for."

"Now that's a phrase I never thought I'd hear come out of your mouth."

They waited as the server cleared their plates.

"But it's true. I do feel sorry for him. When I met him, he was sitting by the window in the Hastings Arms in George Street, and watching the entrance to that bar across from there. I think he might have known that's where Miller goes now. He was waiting to see if Steve and his new girlfriend arrived, which they did, and when I left, he was still sitting there, getting quietly drunk and waiting for them to leave."

"It's like he's been jilted."

"Exactly. And I think that's why he's suddenly so keen to talk to me; he thinks we're both in the same boat."

"But you've never been out with Steve."

"No, but neither has he, it's just that Steve lived for his work and therefore Bob was his main man. Now, all Steve has eyes for is his glamorous girlfriend."

"And Bob has no one and neither do you. No one here, anyway."

They thought about that for a moment.

"Are you going to give him a sympathy fuck then?" Kate asked with a twinkle in her eye and laughed at her friend's horrified expression.

* * *

Monday passed and it was with a sense of relief that there was neither another body nor another confrontation with Dr Grantham. At lunchtime, Callie went to the care home to see Mrs Conway. There had been no further incidents but she wanted to explain to her patient, and the matron, that she had referred her to the falls clinic in the hope that they would be able to get to the bottom of why Mrs Conway was having problems. She was pleased, but surprised, to see that Lewis Conway was already there, visiting his mother.

"Unfortunately, there's quite a long waiting list to be seen at the clinic," she explained to him. "I've told them it's urgent but it could be a while."

"Would it help if she went privately?"

"Well…" Callie was always loath to suggest that patients pay to be seen earlier than they would be on the NHS but in this case, she felt it might be justified. "I could contact the consultant and see if he can see her earlier as a private patient, or if some of the tests could be done before he sees her. I'll let you know."

His attitude seemed very different from the last time she had seen him and she was curious to know why.

"Are you happier with your mother's care now?" she asked.

"Well, at least I know now that she's not being neglected or abused in some way, so yes, I suppose I am, and I'm sorry about what I said when I came to see you."

"No problem – I understand how difficult it is."

She would have liked to know how he knew that about his mother's care, but he hurried away before she could ask.

* * *

Callie finally met up with Jayne in the café by the police station. She was ravenous and was, for once, pleased that the portions were huge.

"Anyone would think you were avoiding the police station." Jayne laughed.

"Well…" Callie laughed too, but they both knew it was true. "I just wondered how things were going."

"To be honest, they're not."

"Oh." That was a bit of a conversation stopper. Callie paused to eat some of her sandwich and think what she could say next. "At least there have been no more bodies."

"Unless there are and no one's found them yet."

Depressing as that thought was, Callie had to concede it was possible. If no one was moving into the property straight away, the cleaning might be left a day or two.

"Nigel's going through all the CCTV in streets around Marine Court and he's identified our man, victim three, weaving his way back from some pub or bar. He was alone and he looked well drunk but there doesn't seem to be anyone following him. There is only one woman a while later, and even she wasn't close to him or anything. Bob Jeffries is asking round pubs in the area trying to see where he might have been to get so drunk."

"What about his blood alcohol level?"

"It was highish, been sent off to check for drugs as well but that will take longer."

"The killer has to make a mistake soon, surely?" Callie felt frustrated. "What's happening with the letting companies?"

"I've checked everyone who rented the three properties," Jayne continued between mouthfuls of her tuna melt panini. "There were none who had rented all three, but twelve people had rented two of them."

"Are you going follow up on them?" Callie asked, resisting the temptation to tell Jayne that she had a thin string of melted cheese hanging from her chin.

"Yup," she replied. "I managed to cross one off the list straight away because she was victim two. Seems she came down to see her gran in the old people's home quite often."

"Well, at least that means only eleven more to go."

"Of which only eight are male and most are based in London, so the Met will be visiting them initially. And there's one in Hampshire I'll be calling later and see if I can persuade the boss to let me go and see him in person. I could really do with a day out after all this time closeted with Nigel going though spreadsheet after spreadsheet of information."

Callie could see her point. Nigel Nugent was only marginally more interesting than a spreadsheet – although he'd probably think that was a compliment.

Jayne's mobile rang just as they were leaving, and she hurried away with a brief apology and mouthing the words: "They've found another body."

As she hurriedly walked back to the surgery, Callie expected her own phone to ring with a request to attend the scene, and she was rehearsing her excuses to Linda and her colleagues, but there was no call.

It wasn't until she was home later that evening and switched on the news, that she understood why. The body of a young man had been found strangled in an apartment in Brighton, not Hastings, and the press had now dubbed the murderer The Seaside Serial Killer.

Chapter 17

According to the papers, The Seaside Serial Killer was now thought to be responsible for a total of six deaths, although as Callie looked at the reported details, she thought that at least one could be discounted because there were more differences than similarities between the cases. Despite her scepticism, the press seemed determined to add every unnatural death in any seaside town – or in one instance, nowhere-near-the-seaside town – to the killer's tally, knowing that the greater the number of bodies the more newspapers they would sell.

"At least that gives them more cases to work on," Linda said, reading over her shoulder in the office.

"Yes, but it may also give them an awful lot of false leads," Callie answered, imagining all the extra work it would take to rule out the random deaths.

One good development was the announcement of a joint task force involving several police forces, set up to try and look at links between all the deaths and decide which were definitely the work of the same killer. Good was probably not the word that either Miller or Jeffries would use, she knew, as they would hate having to liaise with other forces in this way. It was one thing to hand the complete investigation over, but quite another having to conduct your own work with interference from all sides.

Jayne had rung and told her that the Met had said they had spoken to all of the men who had booked two out of three of the holiday lets where the three Hastings bodies were found, and nothing suspicious had been discovered. Alibis had been checked, except that only one of the suspects had one. That person had been abroad on business, Jayne told Callie. It seemed that the other two didn't have anything you could call an alibi as they didn't seem to have thought they might need one. Jayne had herself called the man in Hampshire, and he'd told her he used to meet his girlfriend in Hastings because she lived in Dover and it was about halfway between them. They'd split up before the first murder and he had alibis from his current girlfriend for all three murders.

It wasn't until later, when she was home and discussing the case over the phone with Billy that a thought occurred to her.

"Do you think the killer might not be using his own credit cards to book the places."

"Well, they can't be stolen ones, can they? I mean, that would have been flagged up, surely?"

"Not stolen no, but what if a husband uses his wife's or girlfriend's card, or just a friend's card, something like that?"

After they had said their goodbyes, she gave it more thought. Not wanting to disturb Jayne at home, she rang Bob Jeffries instead.

"Wouldn't a wife notice if her husband was booking trips away on her card and not taking her with him?"

He sounded tired, and perhaps a little drunk, and Callie wondered if it had been wise to call him this late.

"Not if there was a legitimate reason for him to be down here for work or something."

"The murders occurred at weekends."

"True. Or perhaps he could have taken a card out in her name without her knowing, if they have a joint account or something."

To his credit, Jeffries didn't discount the theory out of hand.

"It'll mean a lot more work," he finally said. "Nigel and Jayne will have to check all the bank accounts attached to the cards, see if any are joint ones, or if the names on the accounts the money came out of don't match the booking details."

"And addresses," she quickly added before he put the phone down. "Because they might live together, and email addresses because they could have booked it under the card holder's details but if the email address is—"

There was a groan from the other end of the phone and then the click of Jeffries cutting her off. She knew she was giving them an impossible amount of work, and it would take time to check any links between people who had booked any of the places where victims had been found, particularly if the investigation was being expanded to include further deaths in other locations, but at least they'd have a bigger workforce to use to do it.

The Failed Attempt

They laughed about the press coverage suggesting all these other murders were down to them. They were happy that they had got it so wrong and that it would tie up the police for days, if not weeks, but it also meant that people would become more aware, more on their guard.

The press said the killer was targeting tourists but the police were obviously holding back the detail that all the visitors had been found in holiday lets. It wouldn't be long before someone leaked that detail, or an enterprising journalist ferreted it out. That was why they had chosen a place that was a little more out of the way for their fourth killing, less chance of CCTV picking them up and comparing them to the people seen at the previous locations.

The downside was that they had to travel by car and park quite a long way from the location. It would've been so much easier to use the train but they were worried about being identified as frequent visitors to the town. And how would they get from the station to the location? They could hardly take a taxi. At least they didn't think the police had cottoned on to the possibility of more than one killer.

They finally arrived at their destination, a small cabin in the woods that a nearby farm let out. It advertised a log burner in the living room and a hot tub set in the decking outside so it was fully booked throughout the winter. They had checked. It was just the place for a romantic break for two. They remembered how they had enjoyed the hot tub when they stayed there. It was the same now. A man and a woman were sitting in it, drinking champagne, and kissing in the steamy air.

They watched from a distance, peering through the dense woods, having whispered arguments about whether or not they dared take on two people. It was with a mix of disappointment and excitement that they saw the man stand up. He was naked. He was also well-built and muscular and there was no way they could take him on, not with the woman there as well. Tonight was not going to be a night for killing. They would have to content themselves with watching and, as the naked man sat on the edge of the Jacuzzi so that his girlfriend could take him in her mouth, they moved closer through the dense woods to see better.

It excited them both, this watching, and she undid his coveralls and took him in her mouth, bringing him to swift climax and causing him to cry out. They held absolutely still, frightened to move, to breathe, in case they had been heard. She peered through the undergrowth. The couple in the tub had stopped what they were doing and were looking back at her, at them both, even though the trees must surely be hiding them.

"Who's there?" the man shouted, and grabbing a towel rushed towards the woods.

They ran then, not worrying about being seen. They ran through the trees and bushes, helter-skelter. He didn't follow them for long, his lack of clothes and shoes hindering him. But he must have seen them, in their white coveralls, standing out against the dark of the trees in the night.

Chapter 18

"No more bodies then?" Kate asked when they met in the pub later that week. "Do you think he's moved on to pastures new?"

"I certainly hope so," Callie replied, although a little bit of her didn't agree. If the killer had moved to another area, it would make him that much harder to catch. "But I'm not sure I believe it."

"Watcha, ladies," Bob Jeffries said as he joined them at the table. "Thought I'd find you here."

If Kate was surprised that their regular girls' night out had been gate crashed by a man, and Bob Jeffries at that, she hid it well.

"To what do we owe this dubious pleasure?" she asked as he sat down and placed his pint on the table, indicating that he was staying rather than just saying a quick hello.

"Thought the doc here might want an update," he replied. "That and I was hoping to ask her opinion on something."

Callie raised her eyebrows.

"My opinion?"

"Yeah, if that's okay."

"Of course."

"Well, update first, that's the easy bit. One of the other deaths, in Norfolk, has been discounted. Turned out to be a domestic."

"I thought it didn't sound promising."

"Exactly."

"What about the others?"

"Well…" He hesitated. "The only one that's a real possibility, to my mind anyway, is the one in Brighton. It was in a flat rented out short- term, although not strictly as a holiday let. No sign of a break-in and the bloke was found strangled in bed."

"And the others?"

"Nothing like the same, so I'm discounting them even if the task force leader says we have to keep an open mind."

Jeffries was not known for his open mind, that was for sure.

"You still seem hesitant to include this Brighton one too," Kate said.

"There were some differences from ours. Not least, there was some DNA."

"What from?" Callie and Kate both knew that DNA could be detected in minute samples these days, and not just from blood.

"Semen," Jeffries answered her. "And there is the other big difference, this bloke who was dead, had recently had anal sex."

"Unlike our victims who showed no sign of sexual activity."

"Exactly."

"Were there any marks? Like nail marks on the victim's chest?" she asked.

"You mean, like you said could be a signature or something?"

"Like scratches?" Kate asked.

"No, there seem to be very definite nail marks on the each of our victims, one on the first, two for the— hang on he's numbering them!"

"So there should be four marks on this one if he's connected?"

"Unless we've missed one—" Jeffries paused. "Or more."

It was a sobering thought.

"Well, it's certainly a way we could check if they are the same killer," Callie told him. "We could definitely rule them in if they had marks, but not necessarily out of they didn't, as we don't know it's a signature for sure."

"I'll get Jayne onto it."

"What about Steve, does he think this one is connected?"

"Oh, he and the rest of the senior team are convinced that it is and that it's his first mistake. Believe me, when they find this man's killer, he's going to get charged with all of the murders."

"Unless he can prove unequivocally that it couldn't have been him," Kate, the defence solicitor spoke up.

"Yes," Jeffries agreed. "And he had better have a bloody strong alibi, let me tell you, because they are going to do everything they can to pin them all on him. They are convinced it's the same guy."

"But not you."

"No, if I'm honest and I'm not entirely sure why, apart from the fact that the killer would have to be bloody stupid to leave his DNA like that. I'm sure they'll find other evidence too because he really doesn't seem to have cleaned up the scene at all. It looks like he left in a bit of a panic, and one thing you can say about our killer is that he has shown no sign of being that daft so far."

They all thought about that for a moment.

"Sadly, I agree," Kate finally said and Callie nodded her agreement.

"So, what do we do now?" Callie asked.

"Carry on investigating our three cases as if they are separate from the Brighton victim," Jeffries said.

"Will Steve let you?"

Jeffries looked uncomfortable.

"He doesn't need to know. Most of the team have been pulled off our investigation and are working on the Brighton case as that seems like the best chance of a conviction, but I can still use Nerdy Nigel and Jayne Hale under the radar."

"They don't think the Brighton killer is the same as ours?"

"Well, let's put it this way, they are not totally convinced," Jeffries answered.

Callie nodded. If they were willing to help, it might be enough.

"Are they still going through all the information from the lettings agencies?"

"Yes, but it's going to take a long time to get anything from that."

Callie sighed. She knew he was right.

"What did you want my opinion on? Whether or not the Brighton case was our killer?"

"No, I knew you wouldn't think it was, there are too many differences. What I wanted to ask you, is if you thought our killer could be a woman?"

That surprised her but she gave it some thought.

"It's possible, I suppose, if she was strong enough. None of the victims were particularly large, but the man might have been more of a problem."

"Except he was drunk and drugged."

"Drugged?"

"Well, just a little bit of GHB in his system."

"Enough to make him pass out?"

"Probably not according to the pathologist. The CCTV of him coming back from the pub just shows him to be a bit unsteady on his feet."

"And that would make him easier to overpower which would certainly help if the killer was a woman. What makes you think it might be?"

"I talked to the barman at the pub where the last victim was drinking on the night. He, the barman that is, said the only person who spoke to the bloke was a woman, she bought him a drink too, which was strange cos the geezer was a–" he looked at Callie and Kate and changed his mind about the word he was about to use "–was gay."

"Wasn't there a woman seen on the CCTV footage near his flat too?"

Jeffries nodded and Callie thought about it.

"This is incredibly risky behaviour for a lone woman. It would be very unusual."

"But it's possible?"

"Well, yes, I suppose so. What does Steve think?"

Jeffries snorted.

"He dismissed it out of hand. Told me, well, it doesn't matter what he said. He really doesn't think it could be a woman and he's convinced the Brighton case is going to solve it anyway. End of discussion."

He was obviously hurt by whatever Miller had said to him and was looking for some support, even if it was only from Callie.

"Well, like I said, it's possible, but not likely." This was the best she could do by way of validation for his theory, but it was good enough to bolster his mood and he finished his pint with a flourish.

"Can I get you ladies anything?" he asked and he was almost happy when he left after they had refused his offer.

"Do you really think it could be a woman?" Kate queried after he had gone.

"No, not really, but it's not impossible," she replied but the more she thought about these crimes and how they were being carried out, the more she began to wonder about it. Not a woman on her own, perhaps, but working with a man? Was it possible?

Kate opened another packet of crisps and changed the subject.

"What do you have planned for the weekend?"

"Billy's over."

"Say no more."

"I'm going to have to give our brunch a miss, I'm afraid. We're visiting Billy's family for a lunch that will start early and probably go on all afternoon, if I know them," Callie told her. Billy's family would want time with him, and special meals seemed to go on forever with course after course of home-cooked food, and more people arriving, armed with yet more dishes, at regular intervals.

"After a nice long lie-in, I'll bet," Kate said, winking at Callie.

"What about you? What are you up to?" she asked Kate.

"That's okay, I'm busy too. I'm going to have some me time," Kate answered.

"Who with?"

"Just me," Kate answered with exaggerated patience. "I've got a book, a bottle of wine, and a cabin in the woods. Miles from anywhere."

"Sounds good," Callie said, hesitantly.

"But?"

"No shops? No pub? Why are you going there?"

Kate laughed. "For the peace and quiet."

"I'm not sure I'd enjoy it on my own. Too much nature around," Callie said.

"As far as I know there are no bears in the woods round here."

"But there are other things – foxes, badgers, spiders."

"I'm not frightened by those sorts of things," Kate said. "It's my friend's place, they have a farm and some lodges in the woods, well, two I think and no one's using them this weekend. I've been there before and it's not at all basic, each one has a log fire, hot tub, all the things you would expect from a luxury log cabin. My friend Mike suggested I go there when I said I was a bit fed up after I split up with Diego."

This startled Callie. She had no idea that Kate had split up with the Spanish hunk she had been seeing on and off for a month or two, let alone that she was upset about it. What sort of a friend was she?

"You should have said."

"It happens," Kate replied.

"Are you okay?" she asked as she reached across and took Kate's hand.

"Of course I'm okay!" Kate laughed. "I was glad to see him go. I'm just teasing you. I've got a bundle of work and it will be nice to be able to get on with it. Del and Mike will be at the farm down the road so I'll have dinner with them at some ridiculously early hour because they get up at the crack of dawn, or earlier, and then I'll go back to my rustic log cabin and sit in the hot tub. Imagine it, I can sit in the dark, with a glass of wine, and look at the stars."

"I thought you said it was in the woods?"

"All right, smart-arse, so I'll look at the trees and listen to the owls hooting, the foxes making whatever noise foxes make and spiders crawling up and down the trees in hobnailed boots."

* * *

In the surgery the next day, there was a message from Lewis Conway asking her to call him when she had a moment, but it wasn't until much later in the day when she was able to do so.

"Hello? Mr Conway? It's Dr Hughes here."

"Ah, Dr Hughes, thank you for calling back, I've managed to get an appointment for my mother with the doctor you contacted in the private hospital. It's for next week, so that's much better."

They talked a little about what tests his mother would expect and what the costs were likely to be for those tests under a private doctor and it wasn't until Mr Conway was about to ring off that Callie managed to ask the question she hadn't found time to put to him before.

"Can I ask, how did you know that your mother wasn't being mistreated at the care home, Mr Conway?"

There was a bit of umming and ahing from him before he finally admitted how he knew.

"I installed some hidden cameras," he told her. "I know that's frowned upon, but I read about this family who did that and caught a carer stealing and hitting their mother, so I thought I would do it. I was so convinced something similar was happening to Mum."

Callie decided not to get into a discussion about privacy laws and filming people without their consent, because she could fully understand the reasons why he had taken this step. If she was concerned about a loved one's care, she might well do the same.

"What exactly does the recording show?"

"Her getting up in the night, not even calling for a nurse before she does so, so they aren't ignoring her call bell, and then well, just falling."

"Could I possibly see the recording, Mr Conway?" Callie was suspicious. "People don't generally just fall, not unless there is a reason for it," she explained, "a medical reason, that is."

"Of course, I'll email it to you as soon as I get home, it's on my laptop."

"Thank you."

"But you'll see, she really does just fall, you know, that's the only way to describe what happens. One minute she's standing there, the next minute she's on the floor."

"And you've removed the cameras?" she checked.

"Of course, well, I've switched them off. I did that as soon as I could see that Mum was being well looked after. I can't really remove them, they might think it was a bit off, my taking away her teddy bear clock and the picture of the family in an ornate frame. Especially when I've only just brought them in and made such a fuss about the nurses not touching them."

"I can imagine."

Callie thought about it some more after she put the phone down. Should she warn the home that the cameras were there? She thought not. It could do more harm than good. She would just have to trust that Lewis Conway didn't turn them on again. And what about his story that his mother simply got up and fell over without any real cause? She didn't think it could be that simple; in fact, she was sure that something was happening, the question was: what?

Chapter 19

Callie had managed to get the whole weekend off to be with Billy while he was over. To be fair, with all the extra visits and on-call she had done since Dr Grantham had complained about her attitude and leaving her colleagues in the lurch, she felt she had well and truly done her penance.

Having spent an hour or two in bed as soon as he arrived on the Friday evening, Callie wrapped herself in a bathrobe and sat at the breakfast bar watching Billy cook beef Stroganoff. He had sent her a shopping list in advance so, for once, she had all the ingredients ready. He poured half a pot of cream into the saucepan, and after a moment's hesitation, added some more.

"Got to keep my strength up." He winked at Callie and she felt herself blush as she always did.

"How's Belfast?" Callie changed the subject quickly.

"Good, busy, but very good," Billy replied. "No murders as yet." He sounded almost disappointed. "Unlike here."

"None here for a while, either," Callie corrected him. "Touch wood," she added, hurriedly tapping the table.

"Besides which, I heard on the radio that they've arrested somebody in Brighton for the murders."

"Really?"

"Yes, there was a press conference. It wasn't Steve Miller talking – I rather think he's not part of the top team anymore."

"What did they say? Who have they arrested?"

"They're playing everything very close to their chests. Didn't give any details apart from that a Brighton man aged thirty-seven had been arrested. I daresay more will be slowly leaked over the weekend," Callie said.

"Do you still think they're wrong about the Brighton case?" Billy asked.

"Yes, I'm afraid I do," she replied. "It's just too easy to think that he suddenly got careless and that it's all over." She hadn't heard yet about any marks on the body which rather made her suspect there were none.

"We'll soon know if you're right if there's another killing while he's in custody," Billy said.

"But there haven't been any for a couple of weeks, it seems to have all gone quiet. I'm hoping the killer's been scared off by all this press coverage."

"I sincerely hope so," Billy replied. "We don't want anything to disrupt our weekend."

"So, no more talk mentioning the Q word, just in case." Callie laughed as she touched the wooden table again in the hope it gave her luck and kept the weekend very quiet indeed. "What worries me is that he's tempted to do one now, just to prove that they haven't got the right person in custody."

There was silence as they thought about that.

"You could be right," Billy said sombrely.

* * *

On Saturday afternoon, after they had both had lunch with his parents, Billy went off with his brother to see his cousins. He promised that he would only be away an hour or two, but she knew his family. He would arrive home late in the evening, having eaten vast amounts of yet more food, and fall into bed, exhausted. Having said her thank yous, and made her escape, she drove back to Hastings, leaving him to make his own way back. His brother, or one of his cousins, could drop him back, and she knew it would be quite a bit later.

Still, it meant that Callie had time to check her email and catch up with work. She switched on the news channel, but there was nothing new on the story of the man arrested in Brighton. She knew there probably wouldn't be anything more until the crunch came when they would have to either charge or release him.

If he was the murderer in Brighton, and the DNA and other forensic evidence held up, they could charge him with that and remand him in custody while they searched for evidence for or against him being the Hastings murderer. There was nothing she could do about it, so she turned to her email. True to his word, Lewis Conway had sent her the video file from his hidden camera.

Callie watched the silent black-and-white footage, fast-forwarding to the place he had told her showed his mother's fall. The camera must have been placed high up in the corner of the room by the window as it gave a clear view of the bed, with Mrs Conway in it and the cot sides up to prevent her getting out of bed. She could see the area to one side of the bed, but not the door or far side of the bed. Nothing happened for quite a long while, but as soon as Callie saw movement, she slowed the recording down and backed it up a bit. She watched closely as Mrs Conway sat up in bed and awkwardly tried to rub her foot and ankle. She clearly had cramp or some other pain in her legs that had woken her.

After a while, her discomfort didn't seem to be getting better, so the old lady reached back, unclipped the cot sides and lowered them so that she could get out of bed. Not much of a deterrent, Callie thought, but she was pretty sure that Mrs Conway would not be able to undo them if she was sleepwalking or confused as they were quite fiddly things to loosen.

Mrs Conway got out of bed and stood beside it. She made no effort to put on her dressing gown or slippers, she just stood there and then lent slightly forward. Callie knew that placing your foot flat on a cold floor and stretching the calf muscle often helped to relieve cramp. So far, so easy to explain. Then, very suddenly, Mrs Conway just crumpled onto the floor, knocking her tray table as she did so and sending books and drinks and the call button flying. Once on the floor, she just lay there. Callie watched closely and then backed the recording up and watched again. She hadn't tripped on her slippers or rug, there was no outward warning of what was about to happen at all. Her patient just simply dropped and there was no twitching or signs of rhythmic movement afterwards to suggest a seizure. It looked just like a simple faint, but probably wasn't, Callie knew.

She fast-forwarded again, until she saw Mrs Conway stir, and slowly sit up. A nurse came into the room and hurried over to her, helped her gently back into bed, checking she was unhurt. It looked like the care Mrs Conway was getting was exemplary, but Callie knew the cause of the falls needed further investigation.

The Tiger's Claw

This time, as they watched from the woods, they saw that it was a woman on her own who had rented the cabin. Perfect. They watched as she left, carrying a bottle of wine, and walked towards the farmhouse about half a mile away. It was already beginning to get dark and she had left a light on, the better to find her way back. They were glad they had got to the cabin so early, or they might have missed seeing her.

They watched and waited, making sure that there wasn't anyone else in the place, but there was no sign of movement. Of course, someone might be joining her later, but the fact that the woman had gone out for dinner alone, suggested not.

She turned to him and smiled. This was better, much better than the last time. They would be ready and waiting for their new target to come back from the farmhouse and tonight, they would kill again.

She kissed him, a long, deep, kiss, and she could feel the stirrings of his excitement, too. It was going to be good night.

Chapter 20

Callie had sent an email to Mrs Conway's consultant, explaining what was on the video recording and expressing her concern that the falls were in fact drop attacks. She knew that Mrs Conway would need an EEG to rule out a neurological cause, and she had ordered an ECG to check her heart, but if the attacks were caused by an intermittent heart rhythm disorder, as she suspected, it might require longer term monitoring if they were to catch the specific problem.

She was concentrating so hard on making sure she had done all she could for her patient that it took her a moment or two to realise that her mobile phone was ringing.

"Hello?" she said, checking her watch as she did so. It was far too early for it to be Billy saying he was on his way home.

"Dr Hughes? It's Sergeant Fernandez here, from the custody suite."

Callie had a slight adrenalin rush when she realised it was the police station, but the details were much more mundane than she hoped. They had a prisoner in custody who seemed to be on drugs and was giving them cause for concern. They wanted her to come and assess if said person was fit to be detained or if they ought to transfer her to the local hospital. It was a no-win situation for Callie: the custody sergeant did not want the responsibility of looking after someone who was high as a kite, and the hospital wouldn't want her either. To make matters worse, it was a regular customer of Callie's, both at the police station and at the surgery. Marcy Draper was a local working girl who she had tried to help come off drugs several times now, but her patient's heart wasn't in it and that inevitably meant that, much as she insisted that she wanted to straighten out, she always went back on drugs. Given her job, Callie could understand why. The problem was, when she was high, she was a nightmare, regularly assaulting both her customers and the police.

Callie put on her coat. Billy would be ages yet, so she had plenty of time to check on Marcy and get back before him.

* * *

"What are you like?" Callie chided the young woman slumped in the chair in the examination room.

"I know, I know. I've messed up again, Doc," Marcy replied, her voice slurred.

"Yes," Callie agreed. "You certainly have."

Callie examined Marcy and then told the custody sergeant that she was fit to be detained but not interviewed in her current state.

"Doubt anyone will be doing much interviewing – there's not really much to be gained given the drugs found on her. It's not enough for intent to supply, so it'll just be a slap on the wrist for possession."

Callie made a mental note to follow up and see if she could persuade Marcy to go into rehab again, but she doubted that her patient would want that, even supposing there was a place anywhere. The lack of rehab space was an ongoing problem and why would they waste one on someone like Marcy who didn't really want to give up taking drugs? Sometimes, Callie knew, you just had to take a step back and let people do what they had to do and wait until they were ready to accept your help. If they were ever ready.

It was still only early evening and Callie didn't expect Billy home for another couple of hours yet, so she decided to pop into the incident room. In previous investigations she had worked on, she would have expected Steve Miller, as senior investigating officer, to still be there despite the fact that it was a Saturday evening. However, with this investigation, she suspected that his new girlfriend would have tempted him out of the building by now and she was right.

"Watcha, Doc." Jeffries looked up as she entered the incident room.

"Want a cup of tea?" Jayne Hales asked her.

"Please," Callie answered and looked around the room. Nerdy Nigel the computer geek was there and a few civilian staff were catching up with their paperwork, but otherwise the incident room looked surprisingly quiet.

"The boss isn't here..." Jeffries answered her unspoken question, it seemed that only the dedicated remained to work. "Mind you, I can see his point – we don't seem to be getting anywhere."

Jayne returned with three mugs of tea and a packet of custard creams and they sat down at one of the many free desks. The two detective sergeants seemed happy to take a break from the endless rounds of checking leads and tip-offs.

"What's happening about Brighton?"

"Do you want the bad news or the bad news?" Jeffries asked with his mouth full of biscuits.

"He's not our killer?"

"Give the Doc a prize."

"The suspect has confessed to killing the man there, he left so much evidence there wasn't much else he could do," Jayne explained.

"Lovers' tiff," Jeffries added and couldn't keep a note of distaste from his voice. "Seems there'd been some playing around while they'd been on holiday together in the Canaries and it turned violent. He wasn't even in the country for two of ours. Only got back home last week, so we are back to square one."

"That's a shame." Callie sighed.

"Can't say that we really thought it was the same person," Jayne said.

"And what about the others the task force is looking at? Are they likely to be our killer?"

Jeffries snorted his response and Jayne just shook her head.

"I don't know why they ever thought a task force was going to be any bloody use." There were crumbs down Jeffries' tie and Callie had to resist the urge to brush them off.

"Have you had any useful calls?" Callie asked.

"No," Jeffries replied shortly.

"We've had some funny ones though," Jayne chipped in.

"Better than missing takeaways?"

"There was the couple staying at a luxury lodge in the woods, they were having sex in the hot tub when they were disturbed by a couple of voyeurs."

"Wow! And they rang the tip line?"

"They said they might be connected because one of the news reports said the killer might be wearing forensic coveralls so that he didn't leave any DNA and the pair they chased off were in them."

"In CSI garb?"

"Yeah, weird, right?"

Callie and Jeffries looked at each other, the call was clearly news to him.

"You know what you were saying about it possibly being two people working together?" he said to her.

"And a lodge would be a holiday let, right?" she replied.

"Oh my God!" Jayne said. "You mean you think it could have been the killer or killers? I just thought it was doggers!" She looked horrified that she hadn't seen the connection.

"Where was this lodge?" Callie asked urgently.

"On a farm somewhere just outside Bodiam." Jayne turned to Nigel at his computer and he hurriedly checked.

"Willow Farm, off the B2244."

Callie grabbed her bag.

"Kate's staying at a lodge in some woods by a farm near Bodiam." She hurried to the door, closely followed by Jeffries.

"We'll go in my car," he said. "We'll need the blues and twos."

* * *

Callie tried to call Kate as they sped along the streets of Hastings. She was holding on to the dashboard with one hand to steady herself as they went around a corner and narrowly missed a pedestrian.

"It just goes straight through to voicemail," she said to Jeffries as she tried again.

"Never get a decent signal once you leave town and go out into the wilds."

"Not a fan of the countryside then, are you?" she asked him. It was more for something to say, to take her mind off both his atrocious driving and the worry that Kate might be in danger.

"Once you've seen one field, you've seen them all," he replied. "But no two towns are alike."

She tried to think that one through and had to concede he had a point; she just wasn't sure it was a valid one. She gave up and googled Willow Farm instead and found a landline number to ring.

"Hello? Is that Willow Farm? I'm sorry to disturb you but I'm trying to urgently contact my friend Kate Ward? Yes, yes, that's right, she's staying in one of your lodges, I believe. Yes, it is urgent and I'm sorry if I woke you, but I understand you had some intruders last weekend? At the lodge?"

It took a while for Callie to get any sense of urgency through to the man at the other end of the line. He clearly didn't like being woken up, even though it was only just gone eight in the evening. As he pointed out, repeatedly, he had to be up at four to get the cows in for milking. But she finally did get through to him that she was worried about her friend's safety and that she was on her way, with the police, but could he go and check on her, please? Now? After much grumbling he agreed, but Callie was still worried that he wouldn't get up to the lodge with any great speed.

"We'll probably be there before him." Jeffries had caught on to the problems she seemed to be having and put on a burst of speed that sent Callie lurching into the door again. She clutched hold of the grab handle tightly to try and steady herself while trying Kate's phone again.

They sped up the hill towards Bodiam village and Jeffries swung a right without even slowing down. They raced along the narrow road, passing the castle, pub, and a few cottages and then he slammed on the breaks.

"Bloody hell!" he swore as he backed up and turned into the tiny lane he had missed, his brain having subconsciously registered the sign saying 'Willow Farm and Lodges'.

Thank goodness they were both wearing seat belts, Callie thought as she rubbed her bruised chest.

They tore past the farmhouse where a signpost indicated they needed to turn left towards the lodges. Callie could see the figure of a man and his Labrador walking down the lane, so they had indeed got there before the farmer. They shot past him and into the woods, having to slow a little as the lane narrowed and the trees got closer together. At last, Callie saw Kate's car parked next to a wooden cabin. The lights were on.

Jeffries screeched to a halt as the door of the cabin flew open and two people, dressed in white forensic suits, probably alerted by the strobing blue lights and the siren, rushed out of the cabin and into the woods. Jeffries chased after them as Callie hurried inside. They had very different priorities. The main door led into a small room that was an open-plan kitchen and cosy living room with a log burner. It was empty.

"Kate!" she called out as she hurried through the door at the end into a double bedroom.

Inside she found Kate, fully dressed, sitting on the double bed holding her throat and coughing.

"Are you okay?" Callie rushed to her and put her arms around her.

Kate clung on to her friend.

"They were waiting for me, in here!" she croaked and sobbed and Callie held on to her, rocking her back and forth and saying quiet, comforting words until her friend had herself back under control.

"I tried to scratch them," Kate said, but I couldn't get at their skin, the coveralls and gloves were taped together, so there was no skin to get at!"

"Shh, shh," Callie comforted her. "I know you did your best, it's okay."

Jeffries came back.

"They got away," he said.

The farmer came in as well.

"Everything all right then?" he asked, apparently unaware that anything very dramatic had happened at all.

Chapter 21

Callie insisted that Jeffries arrange for her and Kate to be driven back to her flat as soon as reinforcements and the crime scene techs had arrived and taken over. Kate had agreed to change out of the clothes she had been wearing so that they could be taken for forensic testing; not that anyone expected to find anything. The two killers had been fully kitted out in coveralls, masks, gloves, overshoes, and shower caps to make sure they left no trace of themselves behind.

Callie let Billy know what was happening as they were being driven back in a marked car, and he was ready and waiting for them with a spare quilt to wrap Kate up in. He understood shock, and being thorough, had made hot chocolate and dug out a bottle of cooking brandy from the back of a cupboard as well.

Once Kate was settled on the sofa with her hot toddy, she finally stopped shaking and was able to give her statement to Jayne when she arrived a short time later.

"They were inside the cabin when you got back?" Jayne checked once she had set up her phone to record the interview.

"Yes, there was nothing to warn me, the lights were all off apart from the one on the veranda that I had left on when I went out for dinner."

"And the door was locked?"

"Yes, I remember locking it."

"You are absolutely sure?"

"Yes. I am positive. I checked it when I went out. I told myself I was being silly – who was going to steal anything when I was in the middle of nowhere?" Her voice broke slightly as she said this.

Jayne looked at Callie; they must have copied the key when they stayed there themselves. How else could they have got in?

"And you didn't see anything untoward earlier?" Jayne asked. "Anyone watching the lodge from the woods?"

"No, nothing." Kate shivered at the thought.

"Go on, what happened when you got back?"

"I unlocked the door—"

"The front door?"

"Yes."

"It was still locked?"

"Yes. I would have been suspicious if it wasn't."

These killers weren't stupid, Callie thought, they would know how to make sure their victims suspected nothing was amiss until it was too late.

"So, I opened the door and went into the living area, reaching for the light and pushing the door shut at the same time. I'd closed the curtains before I went out too, so it was quite dark. It was then that I sensed movement, someone must have been behind the door."

"Just one person?"

"At that point, but as soon as he grabbed me—"

"You are sure it was a man?"

"Yes, probably, he was tall, well built, but... it could have been a woman, I suppose, I just assumed..." Kate's voice broke again.

Callie took her hand and gave it a squeeze.

"Go on," Jayne said once Kate had got herself under control again.

"I was struggling and tried to scream, but there was a hand clamped over my mouth, something was round my neck too. That was when I realised that there were two of them. I think the second person had come in from the bedroom. It all gets a bit hazy after that. They kept pulling whatever was round my neck tighter and I blacked out."

"And they were both doing it?"

Callie knew that was important.

"Absolutely. This wasn't one of them doing it while the other reluctantly watched. They were both very much involved."

"What happened next, do you remember?"

"Not really, I think they carried me into the bedroom, but I was pretty much out of it and when I came to, I was on the bed and they were back to strangling me. I tried to fight back but I must have blacked out again. The next thing I knew, I was coming around and Callie was there. I've never been so pleased to see anyone in my life." She sobbed and Callie held her as Jayne stopped the recording and collected up her things.

"Have they found anything at the cabin?" Callie asked quietly as she showed Jayne out.

"The CSIs are still checking but it looks like they had a car which they had parked about a quarter of a mile away, we think. There are tyre tread marks in a rarely used gateway there and they are pretty sure the footprints lead to it. It's hard to be certain because of all the undergrowth and that, but it looks that way." Jayne looked at Callie, she was clearly upset. "I'm sorry, I just feel so awful, if only I'd realised and brought that call to the boss's attention—"

"How could you have known?" Callie did her best to console the detective sergeant, although privately she felt that Jayne should have at least realised it was suspicious. "And we frightened them into making a mistake or two, footprints, not obscuring their tyre tracks, and there might be more. You never know, something like that might just be the lead that breaks the case."

Jayne didn't seem to think this was likely.

"Bit of a long shot, but they did leave a plastic overshoe in one of the muddier spots, we think, so we have that and also managed to get impressions of a woman's left trainer."

"You see? It all helps. They have to be getting all this stuff from somewhere – maybe you can find out where?" They both knew this was unlikely; so many places sold coveralls and shoe covers, and all of the protective clothing they had been wearing, and the situation had only got worse since Covid. But Callie was refusing to be disheartened. "Plus, we now have another location where we can trace back and see who has been there before. And the close call will stop them trying again for a while at least, you mark my words."

She wasn't sure she believed that, and Jayne didn't look as though she did either, but it was something to hope for. Nearly getting caught must have put the wind up them at the very least; she just hoped that didn't excite them even more and make them want to take the risk again.

* * *

The next morning, Callie crept around the flat, leaving Kate asleep on the sofa. It had been very late before they had persuaded her to get some rest and been able to go to bed themselves. Billy was asleep too, but she left a note letting them both know that she was just going to the police station to collect her car and would be back soon. She knew she was leaving Kate in safe hands. Billy would look after her.

It was a cold, bright morning for once, and she bought a cup of tea and a pain au chocolat to go at the bakery in the High Street, and ate her breakfast as she walked along the seafront to the police station.

Rather than just take her car and go home, she went up the stairs to the incident room, hoping to find out more about how the investigation was moving forward now that they had more to go on. She also wanted to thank Bob Jeffries and make sure Miller knew just how vital his help had been.

She wasn't surprised to find that the incident room was much busier and there was more of a sense of purpose about the way people were working.

She waved a hello to Jayne and Nigel, although she didn't think he noticed because he was staring at his computer screen and scrolling backwards and forwards, checking information.

Jayne was standing by the whiteboards at the front of the incident room. They already had a lot more information on them and she was adding yet more. Callie could see that there was now space for two murderers, unidentified male and unidentified female, and some photographs of the new location were already up there. She shuddered as the reality of how close a call it had been hit home.

Miller and Jeffries were in the office, having a heated discussion, which seemed the norm these days, and Callie made her way over and knocked on the door before entering.

"Good morning," she said to Jeffries and he nodded in reply. "Thank you so much for your help last night," she said. "If I'd gone on my own, I hate to think what might have happened. I would probably have been too late and Kate would be dead, I mean it, you were fantastic."

"That's okay," he said gruffly. "I wanted to get there quickly as much as you."

Embarrassed by her thanks, he went out and left her with Miller. She turned on him.

"And no thanks to you."

He looked surprised.

"I wasn't here," he said.

"Exactly, you weren't here. Not that you would have been much use if you were. You have managed to be mentally absent even when you have been physically present for the whole of this investigation."

"That's not fair." He had flushed a nasty shade of red. He looked haggard, as if he wasn't getting enough sleep, but it wasn't work that was keeping him awake, she was sure.

"Isn't it? If you had been doing your job you might have spotted that report and put two and two together before Kate got attacked, but as it is you are worse than useless and I blame you that my friend nearly got killed." She realised she was shouting and that everyone in the incident room was looking at the office. She was pretty sure she was only saying what they were all thinking. "Pull yourself together before anyone else gets killed," she hissed at Miller and went out, head held high.

She got smiles and surreptitious nods from everyone in the incident room as she walked through and as she passed Jeffries, he silently clapped and grinned at her. They all seemed to understand, and approve of, her outburst.

* * *

Callie felt that it was now only a matter of time before they identified the two killers. It had to be, surely? She hoped that their close call would mean they waited before killing again, but she also didn't want them to run, pack up their house or houses and go abroad – although that was exactly what she would do in their situation. They must know that they would be identified soon, unless they seriously underestimated the police.

She tried not to think about the fact that it was a lack of ability and commitment from the police that had meant they had succeeded in eluding capture for so long. Or, more specifically, Miller's lack of attention to the investigation. She wondered how he must feel, knowing that the blame for the continued killing spree had to, in part, be laid at his door.

Once Callie was back at the flat, Kate said that she wanted to go home. She needed the familiarity and comfort of her own place and insisted that she was fine. She was clearly worried that she was in the way and knew Billy and Callie would want some time together, despite their insistence that it wasn't so.

Finally giving in when Kate threatened to call a taxi, Callie drove her to the small terraced house, parked on double yellow lines outside and followed her in.

"I'm absolutely fine," Kate insisted again and she did sound much better, her voice was no longer so hoarse and the bruising to her throat was not so obvious.

"I'll just make you some tea." Callie went towards the kitchen.

"No." Kate stopped her. "I can do that, just go and enjoy what's left of your weekend."

"Are you sure?"

"I'm going to have a long hot bath, wrap myself in a duvet and lie on the sofa watching mindless TV and eating chocolate and no, I don't want an audience."

"Sounds good." Still, Callie hesitated. "I'll call this evening."

"Good. Now go."

Callie left her and returned to Billy, to spend some time with him before he had to leave for Belfast again. The trouble was, she found it hard to stop thinking about all that had happened, and what might have been, so Billy suggested a walk along the cliff path to clear her head and she readily agreed.

It was a fine but windy autumn day, just right for blowing away any cobwebs. They stopped at the top of a steep climb to catch their breath and Billy pulled her close and kissed her.

"I love you, you know."

"I do know, and I love you too," she replied as he kissed her again.

"We could get married," he started, but stopped as he felt her stiffen. "I'm not putting any pressure on you, we can carry on like this as well, for as long as you like," he added quickly.

She relaxed a little, while he waited with bated breath.

"I'll give it some thought," she conceded. "But if you think you are going to get away with a proposal like that, you can think again, Dr Iqbal." She laughed. "I want the exotic location, bended knee, diamond ring, the works."

He laughed too, from relief.

"So, it's not a 'no' then?"

"No, it isn't," she replied slowly, realising as she said it that she did want to marry this wonderful, thoughtful, kind man; she just wasn't sure she wanted to live with him. "But I do need more time."

He nodded his understanding and grinned.

"Right, I'll get planning then. Exotic location it is."

Chapter 22

On Monday morning, Billy got up before dawn to get to Gatwick for the early flight to Belfast. He tried hard not to disturb Callie, but she was awake and once he was gone, she couldn't get back to sleep. Too many things were going through her mind: the way Miller had failed to take control of the investigation, the subsequent attack on Kate, Billy's proposal; so many things had happened over a short weekend. Realising that further sleep was out of the question, she got up and made herself some tea.

She sat at the small dining table by the window and looked out over the town as the sun rose. She loved this view and how it changed with the seasons and the weather. As she watched the town wake up and come alive, she thought about her future.

Did she want to marry Billy? Yes, she did, but the move to Belfast, and the worry about her future work, meant that it wasn't as simple as that. What would have happened to Kate if she hadn't been here, in Hastings? Whilst she thought it unlikely that her friend's life would be in danger again, at least she hoped not, she wasn't sure she wanted to leave her, or the police, or the surgery. Not to mention her parents, who weren't getting any younger and would likely need more support as time went on.

With a sigh, she finished her tea and headed for the shower. This wasn't a problem that she could answer just yet, so it would have to wait.

* * *

When she was doing her admin at the end of her morning clinic, she was pleased to see a reply from Mrs Conway's consultant. He had called their patient in to see him and, having seen the recording of a 'fall' that Callie had sent him, apparently agreed with her suspicions that these were drop attacks rather than falls and that her heart rhythm needed to be investigated. He had organised the EEG in case the falls had an epilepsy type of cause, but was leaning towards the answer coming from the 24-hour ECG monitor he had fitted. If neither of those captured any results, he would get a loop recorder fitted so that her heart rhythm could be monitored longer term. He suspected that she would need a pacemaker, but was reasonably confident that he could get to the bottom of her problem and fix it. Exactly what Callie thought was needed, so she felt pleased with both his response, and that she had been right in the first place.

Her visit list was longer than usual because Dr Grantham was taking another personal day. Try as she might, she wasn't able to get any more information than that from Linda.

"If he wanted you to know what was going on, he would have told you," the practice manager replied when Callie tried to pump her for more information, which was undeniable, but frustrating all the same.

He was in his late fifties now and she wondered if he was ill, or if he might be considering retirement. Either thought was unsettling, much like Billy's proposal.

* * *

Dr Grantham remained off work for several days and Callie had no chance to get to the police station, or even arrange a meet-up with Jayne until Wednesday lunchtime. The morning should have been Callie's admin time so she had no surgery booked, but she had spent the entire session catching up with overdue visits so that her colleagues would not have to do too many. She hoped she had gained a lot of brownie points for doing this, but suspected no one would actually notice her heroic efforts, except for Linda. Linda had promised to get in some extra chocolate biscuits if Callie helped out, and there was little Callie wouldn't do for a plain chocolate digestive.

"Hiya," she said to Jayne as she arrived at The Goat Ledge café, which was made up of a group of colourfully converted beach huts on the front in St Leonards.

Callie was tired and just a little fractious. Some of the visits had been particularly challenging, and some were just a waste of her time. She had decided against either visiting the incident room or going to the café near the station because she really didn't want to see Miller again after giving him a piece of her mind and she had persuaded Jayne that a longer walk for her lunch would do her good, not to mention that the food was better at the Goat Ledge.

Jayne had already got them a table by the window and was busy looking at the menu.

"Hiya, I fancy a classic fish bap and some chips," she said as Callie arrived. She was clearly in a hurry to get back.

"With or without katsu sauce?" Callie asked.

"Without."

Callie placed the order: two fish baps, one chips, no sauce and two teas, before getting down to business.

"Have you made any progress?" she asked.

"Yes, and no," was the reply. "We have narrowed our search down to three possibles, although we haven't finished going through all the information yet, so there could be more."

"Three couples?"

"Well, they are not couples, but three possible pairs of renters who have used all four locations."

"Did they all use the same agency?"

"No, it's a bunch of different ones."

"What about alibis? Can you discount any of them because they were out of the country or something?"

"We're working on that, but it takes time and, of course, if one has an alibi, we can probably rule out the person they would have to be pairing with to have visited all four."

"Only probably?"

"Well, we don't know that two people were there in all the cases. Nigel and I will carry on trying to trace as many potential suspects as possible, whilst the rest of them will trek round trying to interview and eliminate everyone."

"Miller isn't leaving that to other forces like the Met again?"

"No, no, don't worry." She gave a Callie a small smile. "I rather think that pep talk you gave him means he is going to do everything properly now."

Callie was relieved to hear that.

"And once you think you might have a positive lead, what then? How will you have enough evidence for an arrest, let alone actually charge them?"

"It's not going to be easy," Jayne admitted. "There's still pretty much zero forensic evidence, what with the efforts they've made to leave no trace. We only have the shoe print and a car tyre pattern. There was nothing on the shoe cover and your friend Kate couldn't really give us a good description as they were totally kitted up and masked, with gloves and all that. All we can do is hope that one of them says something incriminating in interview. Like that's going to happen," she added, pessimistically.

Callie knew that it was unrealistic to imagine either of the killers would confess to their crimes when they had taken such care to make sure they would not be caught. The sort of killers that went to the lengths that these two went to, like taping the join between their coveralls and gloves and wearing face masks, were not going to be easy to catch. Not yet, not before they killed again and maybe made more mistakes. Or not.

"Let's hope something more helpful is found, somewhere." Callie tried to sound hopeful, but failed. She sat for a while after Jayne had left, looking at the sea and drinking tea, and thinking. She had the germ of an idea, but couldn't quite see how it would work. It wasn't until later, when she talked things over during her daily phone call with Billy, that it began to present itself as a definite plan or, at least, a possible idea that might develop into a plan. She needed to think it through, and she needed more information from Jayne and Nigel on the number of suspects and any further places that they had rented between them. Places that hadn't yet been used as kill sites.

But she didn't mention it to Billy because she wasn't sure Miller would agree to it, and there was no way she was going to do this without his support, or at least some back-up, and she knew Billy would worry that she would do something stupid. Which she wouldn't, of course, but it would be easier to ask forgiveness than permission. Particularly if the permission was unlikely to be granted.

Chapter 23

Asking Miller to meet her that evening in The Stag was a real test of his promise to take his job more seriously.

"I've got to leave by seven thirty," he said brusquely as he sat down with his pint. "What's this about?"

Jeffries hurried over as well, and sat beside his boss, keen not to be left out of the discussion.

"How are you getting on with narrowing the field of suspects?" Callie asked.

"Fine."

"Badly," Jeffries contradicted his senior officer.

"But you have three couples, or rather pairs of people that have rented all four of the places between them?" She had managed to get as much out of Jayne earlier, but what she really wanted was the details of all of them so that she could memorise their faces. She wanted to be able to recognise them if they were walking down the street, buying groceries or sitting next to her in the pub. She couldn't help a swift glance around at her fellow drinkers as she thought about it.

"Yes." Again, it was Jeffries who answered her.

"And did any of them stay at any other locations? Ones that haven't already been crime scenes?"

There was a moment of silence as they both mulled that over.

"You're thinking they might carry on? Even after the last fiasco?" Miller didn't sound like he believed it. Perhaps he just didn't want to.

"I can't see them stopping, or at least, not for long." She was sorry to say this, but she had to make sure they were prepared.

Miller washed his face with his hands, he really, really didn't want this to be true.

"I think in one case, the answer is no," he said finally. "That's it for one of the pairs, but the other two yes, they had stayed elsewhere."

"How many?"

"That, I can't say for sure, but I'll get Nigel on it tomorrow. I think it's only one or two each."

"So that gives possibly two or a maximum of four locations they might use moving forward."

"Provided our killers are among these pairs." Trust Miller to pour cold water on her idea. "We may have ruled the Brighton death out of our group, but there are still the other two murders, in Suffolk and Surrey, and if they are linked, then none of our pairs are involved, because they've never been to either place."

Jeffries snorted at this.

"I don't believe for one moment that you really think those deaths have anything to do with ours," she told him, firmly. "And what if one of those pairs Nigel and Jayne have so carefully put together – after many, many hours of work, I might add – what if one of those pairs is responsible for all of these killings and what if they are busy planning the next one? Are you just going to let it happen?"

Both Jeffries and Callie stared at Miller, waiting for his response. He shifted uncomfortably and took another sip of his beer.

"What else can I do?"

"You can watch the other places, wait for them to strike and catch them in the act."

Jeffries looked surprised, and then smiled. Callie, still watching Miller intently, sat back waiting for his reaction.

"Do you honestly think I have that sort of manpower at my command? Enough people to watch four different locations for goodness knows how long? The super would have a fit if I even suggested it."

He had a point.

"But you could narrow it down, guide them to one location."

"How?" Jeffries was interested, even if Miller wasn't.

"We know they tend to back off if more than one person is staying there, and obviously if a place is empty, that won't work for them, so just make sure that every location is either full of groups or couples or empty, except the one you want them to go to, the one that you are watching."

"We could have a team in there waiting for them." Jeffries was positively enthusiastic about the idea.

"You'd have to be careful. They must watch the locations, suss them out before they go in, and you don't know how long they watch for – you mustn't do anything to alert them." Callie wanted them to exercise caution, but Jeffries wasn't going to be dissuaded.

"We could do it, boss, we could catch them in the act." He was really pumped by the thought.

"Just hold on," Miller cautioned. "We need to think it through, look at all the permutations. We couldn't watch more than one place at a time and even that for a limited period. What if we pick the wrong couple's rental history? We'll end up with nothing."

"But meanwhile," she said, "no one would have been killed, if you have blocked out the others."

"We'd need the cooperation of the owners."

"I think they would all jump at the chance of helping to catch this pair. Business has been seriously affected and they will want it over so they can get back to normal."

"And we could see if there is one place that more than one of the couples have been to," Jeffries reasoned. "If there is, then that's the one to go for, and make sure the killers choose it too."

"There might not be," Miller said, "and even if there were, the logistics might still prove hard – what if it's a top floor flat or something? Hard to do it safely."

"Oh, for God's sake, boss," Jeffries exploded. "This is the best idea anyone's put forward by a country mile – just stop being so fucking negative!"

Callie couldn't help but smile at the shocked silence that followed this outburst, even though she hated the fact that everyone in the pub was staring at them.

* * *

A short while later, both policemen had left and she had been joined by Kate, who dumped her coat and bag and sat down while Callie went to the bar to get them both a drink.

"Genius," she said when Callie had told her about the earlier meeting and sketched out her plan. "It could really work."

"I sincerely hope so."

"I really don't want anyone else to go through this." Kate pointed to the scarf around her neck that was hiding the bruising left from her attack.

"Nor do I! Is it still painful?"

"Not really. If I could pass the marks off as love bites, I'd leave my neck uncovered, but I've already had a vicar stop me in the street to slip me his phone number and tell me that if I want to talk, any time, night or day, he'd listen."

"Well that was nice of him."

"It was. I didn't have the heart to tell him I hadn't really tried to kill myself."

"Can I ask you something?" Callie said, uncertain of how exactly she should put it.

"What?" Kate replied.

"Do you have any marks? On your upper breast?"

Kate looked shocked.

"Well, now you mention it, yes. But look—"

She pulled her jumper down slightly and Callie could see five nail marks, not in a line, as the pathologist had described on the male victim's body, but in a curve.

"Do you mind if I?" she gestured with her phone.

"Fire away," Kate replied and Callie carefully photographed the marks.

"It can't be numbering his victims, because then I would have four marks, not five."

"Unless we've missed a victim somewhere."

Kate shuddered, but Callie knew that she hadn't said anything that her friend wasn't already thinking.

Callie hurriedly put her phone away because they were getting funny looks from the other people in the pub, and the barman.

"Do they have any more on the people they think might be involved?" Kate asked, changing the subject.

"They've narrowed it down to three pairs of people, or possibly only two, who could potentially be working together, but none of them have alibis. Seems it was a good night on television. There's nothing to even indicate that they know each other and, according to Jayne, none of them have records. They've all been interviewed, by Sussex officers, but nothing comes up that suggests any of them might be serial killers."

"Not even an inkling? Or a hunch?"

"Well, of course, but their guts all lead them to suspect different people, including some that have been categorically ruled out already."

Kate sighed.

"I just want this to end. Feel safe again, you know?"

"I do, I understand completely." Callie reached out and took her friend's hand. "They really have narrowed it down to just a few people."

"I know. Jayne came around with some photos, but what can I say?" She shrugged. "It's hard to pick someone out when you only saw them with masks and protective glasses on."

Callie patted her hand consolingly.

"They'll get them, I'm sure they will."

"I honestly hope so, but the truth is, I don't exactly relish the idea of a trial. How many times have I had to talk victims into giving evidence? It's hard, Callie, standing up there, whilst the defence counsel pulls your evidence to shreds and trashes your reputation to boot."

"I know, but if the police catch them in the act, they might plead guilty."

"No chance. I don't want to pour cold water on your plan, but even if you have actually persuaded Miller, and he manages to convince the powers that be to let him do it, which I sincerely doubt, our mate Miller isn't going to let them actually start to strangle anyone. You see, if it all works, he's only going to catch them in the act of breaking into the property, and you can bet that they'll only admit to burglary or something. And there isn't any forensics of any note to pin the other murders on them – these two aren't amateurs, Callie – they'll fight tooth and nail to stay out of jail."

Depressing as that thought was, Callie knew she was right. They would.

* * *

"Just don't you volunteer to be the bait," Billy said when she told him about her plan that night.

"Of course I won't," she replied, but at the same time acknowledging to herself that he knew her all too well. "And even if I did, you can bet that Miller will have a whole load of sturdy scrum-half types planted in the bathroom and everywhere just to make sure whoever it is, is safe."

"Just promise me it won't be you."

"I promise," she said, and didn't even cross her fingers as she said it. She had seen the bruises on Kate's neck and the marks on her breast and she had no wish to put herself in line for that. It had been far too close for comfort.

"Billy, did I tell you about the marks the killers have been leaving on the victims?"

"Marks? No, what sort of marks?"

"They look like they are done with the fingernails, but through gloves as there is no DNA."

"What do the marks look like?" he asked. "Are they identical?"

"No, all different, I can send you pictures." She hastily forwarded him the photographs. "I thought he was numbering them, you know one, two, etc., but Kate's got five marks."

"Which would mean one victim was missing."

"Yes."

There was a moment's silence as Billy looked at the photos.

"Weird," he said.

"That's exactly what Bob Jeffries said," she complained. "Do you have any idea what they mean?"

"Nope, no idea, but leave them with me, I'll do some research."

"Thank you. Did I tell you that you are wonderful?"

"Not today."

She could hear the smile in his voice.

"Oh, and, er—" He seemed unusually unsure of himself which alerted Callie immediately. "There's a practice in the city centre that's looking for a new GP partner."

Callie froze; she knew exactly where this was going.

"I'm not trying to put any pressure on you, it's just that it's a really lovely practice and I think you'd get on well with them. You don't have to apply, I'm just going to email you the details so that you can think about it, okay?"

"Okay." She couldn't hide her lack of enthusiasm from him. "Actually, I think I've already seen their advert in GP magazine."

"You saw it? That's good. I'm not trying to rush things or push you into applying, I promise. I just happened to spot the advert on the local medical intranet and thought that it was too good an opportunity to miss."

Callie didn't believe that for a moment; she was caught between being flattered that he was so desperate for her to come and join him that he was looking for jobs for her, and irritation that he was doing exactly that. She was quite capable of getting her own work, thank you very much.

Despite Billy changing the subject and talking about her next visit to see him, trying to plan it, telling her about a new restaurant he had found, their conversation remained stilted, even when they said goodbye.

Callie tried to analyse why she was so upset that he had told her about a job that would mean a move to Belfast. After all, wasn't that what married couples did? Lived together? In the same town or city? It was just that she didn't feel ready, and didn't like him trying to get her to move faster than she was prepared to. Equally, she knew that if he didn't job hunt for her, and push her to apply, she might never get around to it herself.

She checked her inbox and saw that Billy had indeed sent the details to her. She would take a look at them tomorrow, she promised herself, and Billy, silently.

Chapter 24

Callie had no idea if Jeffries would be able to persuade Miller to go ahead with her plan, or whether Miller would, in turn, be able to persuade the superintendent, so she held off as long as possible before calling Jayne.

"Well, hello, Dr Hughes," Jayne answered. "Have you come up with any more bright ideas?"

Her tone was ever so slightly barbed and Callie could understand why. Her plan, if it was ever to move forward, would have triggered a lot of work for the sergeant and her assistant.

"Sorry about that. Do I take it you are still busy checking out the other possible locations?"

"Yes, and Bob Jeffries is visiting them as we find them, trying to see which of them might be suitable, so that we can narrow down the possible locations still further."

"That's excellent news."

"Is that Callie?" she heard Miller say in the background.

"Yes, boss," Jayne replied and after a pause, it was Miller who took over the conversation.

"Callie, the super has asked that we have medical back-up available for this operation, ideally an ambulance nearby, but I don't want it too close, in case it spooks our subjects. So I suggested having you there. Any chance you could make yourself available? Not in the house, but with the surveillance team in a van? Plus, we'd obviously have the ambulance and a paramedic or two a few streets away."

"Of course." Callie jumped at the chance. If she was in the surveillance van rather than the flat, she'd be quite safe and Billy couldn't really complain about that, could he?

"Thanks. I'll leave Jayne to give you the details, once we know where we're going to be." There was a pause as he handed the phone back to Jayne.

"Hi, Doc, it's me again, I take it you agreed?"

"Yes, I'm very happy to be in the van," she replied. "Do you have any idea when this will be? I take it it's just going to be weekend night times?"

"Yes, the theory is that, once they know it's a single person staying there, and that person goes out, they gain access to the property, like they did with Kate, so we'll keep the surveillance going from when the undercover officer goes out until midnight."

"Don't forget that with the one man, they followed him to the pub and she even spiked his drink."

"I know, so that's why we've decided on a single woman as the lure. They haven't felt the need to drug any of the women."

"That's a lot to ask of anyone – being the bait, I mean."

"Needs must and we hope to start this weekend."

"That's quick."

"The boss doesn't want to risk the super changing his mind, and one or two of the owners are kicking up a bit of a fuss about us asking them to cancel anyone who's already booked in locations we don't think would work for surveillance. So we don't want this going on too long."

"It might take a few weeks," Callie said. Not wanting to dampen the enthusiasm, but wanting them to be prepared for a long haul.

"I know, but equally, it might be this weekend, you never know. The owners would be very happy if we caught them quickly."

"We all would be, even though I can't believe it will cause too many cancellations if it goes on anyway. I don't imagine a lot of people are eager to come to Hastings under the current circumstances."

"No, most of the rental locations are empty," Jayne said, "but you'd be surprised to know how many are still taking bookings – mainly people who want to see the town where the killings are taking place."

"I hope they've all increased their security, you know, changed the locks or whatever."

"You'd think so, wouldn't you, but I'm not convinced."

"Well," Callie said, "let me know the when and where once it's all been decided."

"Will do."

* * *

The call back was sooner than Callie had expected and she was invited to attend a planning meeting that evening in the incident room. Jayne told her that the location had been chosen and everything had been set up for that weekend, just as Miller wanted. Due to her sterling work doing extra visits and on-call for all the partners, Callie had a second weekend off in a row. She knew she would have to negotiate with her colleagues if this went on for longer; not something she was looking forward to doing.

When she got to the incident room, it was packed with more people than she had ever seen there before. Some were in uniform; there was a mix of police, ambulance service and, Callie was startled to see, Chris Butterworth from the fire service. He was standing at the back, leaning against the wall and looking as surprised to be there as she was to see him. Quite rightly, Miller seemed to be making sure he had all his bases covered with this operation.

At the front of the room there were some boards, and Callie wandered over to have a look at the pictures on them. On the first there were the images of two men and two women. These must be the pairs of visitors that the team thought could be responsible for the murders. She knew that none of them had rented all the locations, except when viewed in these pairs. She looked at all the Post-it Notes around the individual pictures but could see nothing to say they had been linked in any other way. The images were all taken from social media; it was clear that none of them had records so there were no mugshots for them. She looked more closely at the pictures, hoping for something, anything to stand out, but they all looked like very ordinary people.

Sandy was a pert brunette, twenty-eight years old and a receptionist in a beauty salon in South London. She was paired with Rico, in his thirties, an engineer from Barking. They looked an unlikely pair, but not as unlikely as Beth, a tall, blonde, and leggy accountant from Crawley who was paired with Paul, a forty-something civil servant, who did stand out when she examined his photo, mainly because he was the only one not smiling. It looked as if the picture was taken from his workplace website because he was wearing a suit and tie. Perhaps he didn't do Facebook or Instagram. Or maybe he always wore a suit and tie, even at home.

"Right!"

The general hubbub died down as Miller stood at the front and started speaking. He looked worn out, Callie thought as she moved to the side, and then inched further back into the crowd, so that she was no longer the focus of attention.

"Thank you all for coming here this evening. The purpose of this meeting is to plan an operation set for this weekend." Miller proceeded to speak about practicalities, pointing to a large map that had been placed next to the whiteboards to show where he wanted the ambulance and

159

surveillance vehicles parked. "Chris?" He turned to the fire officer. "If you could be there" – he pointed to the rear of the building marked as the target – "by the embankment, with a light rescue vehicle, and also have a truck with ladders parked nearby, just in case we need any logistical support with evacuations, access, that sort of thing."

Butterworth nodded; it seemed he'd already discussed the operation with Miller and agreed. Callie hoped that didn't mean the location they had decided on was the top floor in a block of flats or something equally awkward.

Miller continued to brief individual units and he projected a series of images of the location onto a screen. Callie was relieved to see it was one of a terrace of cottages backing on to the railway line.

"It's not ideal," Miller went on to inform the group, "because of the houses on either side, plus there is a back way out on to the railway tracks."

Callie thought it was a shame that the cabin in the woods had already been used, because that would have been an ideal location to stake out – easy to ensure it was surrounded, although it would have been very hard to hide everyone in the woods and out of sight of the killers. Callie almost giggled as she had a mental image of Jeffries in full camouflage gear, with a helmet covered in ferns and twigs and with his face painted in black and green stripes like you see in war films. She put a hand over her mouth and managed to stop herself in time. She glanced surreptitiously round hoping her laughter hadn't been spotted, and it looked like she was in luck.

She looked again at the cottages that had been chosen. They really weren't ideal, but going back to a previously used location wasn't an option for the killers because they were likely to have changed their locks after they had been used the first time round. The phrase 'locking the stable door after the horse has bolted', once again came to mind. With all the publicity around the killings, Callie hoped everywhere had changed their locks, whether they had been used for a killing or not, but she suspected that there were still some places where that hadn't happened, and never would.

"It's a bit of a steep drop down to the line," Butterworth commented as the pictures of the back of the property came up. "Could be tricky if they try and escape that way."

"Yes, which is why I don't want them doing that. It would cause havoc to the trains if we had to chase them along the line, which is why we will have officers positioned here" – he tapped the far side of the back wall that separated the small courtyard garden from the embankment – "and here." He pointed to a further location. "Jack, will you make sure that's covered?" He looked at a uniformed inspector who Callie didn't know, who nodded and made a note. "And the back-up van needs to be here, along with the ambulance." The places on the map that he indicated seemed rather a long way out to Callie, but she supposed they had to be, in case they were seen and frightened the subjects away. "The surveillance van will be here, at the end of the street and once the officers are in place" – he looked at Callie – "they won't be able to leave until stood down."

Great, thought Callie, I had better not have too much coffee beforehand. She had heard tales of officers using bottles and such like to relieve themselves when on surveillance, but there was no way she was going to be doing anything so undignified. She would just have to hold it in.

"We need to be in place by 17.30. Most of the murders have occurred on the Saturday night, but just in case, we have organised for all the possible locations to be empty on the Friday as well, including ours. Jayne, our decoy, will arrive at the location, go in and make out like she is staying there, and then, at 18.30, she will leave and walk to The General Havelock pub, where she will spend a couple of hours with two mates, constables Adeola and Whiting."

He looked round and they waved acknowledgment as he said their names, well aware that they had the plum roles for the evening. "Jayne will be tracked as she walks back by officers in cars here and here – Ben and Nigel, that's you two. We are hoping that our subjects will have let themselves into the property and the operation will be over by then, but if not, Jayne will go back to the house and we'll end the operation at 2 am, ready to go again Saturday night. Any questions?"

There were many, all of an operational nature, people wanting to know exactly where and when they had to be in their places, and what to do in the event of various occurrences, some possible and others really, really unlikely, but Callie knew that the unforeseen happened quite often, and it was best to be as prepared as possible.

Once most of the questions had been answered and the meeting had dispersed into small groups, each discussing their particular role, Callie made her way over to Jayne.

"You ended up with the short straw, then," she said with a smile. "How did that happen?"

"I volunteered," Jayne replied with a grin. "Chance of a lifetime."

Callie wondered what her husband thought about her volunteering for a role like that, or whether he had any say in the matter. She rather thought not, which was fair; she doubted if many of the male officers would have asked their wives about taking on a decoy job like that.

"Let's hope it's all over in one night, though," Jayne added. "Don't want to miss too many bedtimes."

Callie thought that was unlikely to happen. Striking lucky on the first attempt would be almost impossible. The dates of the four incidents – or five if you counted the couple caught watching the cabin – meant that the perpetrators had only missed two weekends since the start of their campaign, but last time they had been close to being caught, which must surely make them pause and reassess their chances of remaining free. They could give up altogether, or, more likely, change tactics. That, plus the fact that the police were only watching one location, which might or might not have been visited by the killers, or could possibly have only been visited by the innocent pair still on the shortlist, meant that Callie thought it could take a while before they got it right and caught the killers in the act.

"Might've been better if they could cover two locations at a time, but the super refused. There just aren't enough people and he didn't want to take the chance of spreading them too thinly." Jayne had obviously read her mind.

"Can't argue with his logic. Have they made sure everywhere else is empty, in case?"

"Yup, that's their only option." Jayne nodded to the picture of the terraced cottage still projected onto the screen at the front of the room.

"Let's hope they know that, then," Callie said.

"We'll have a very boring weekend if they don't."

Jayne grinned and Callie sighed. She really didn't want that to happen.

* * *

"And you will be well out of the way?" Billy asked anxiously when she told him about the plans later that evening.

"Absolutely," she replied. "I wouldn't want to be Jayne, even though she gets to spend most of the evening in the pub with a couple of mates, but the thought of going into the place when she gets back…"

"But if the suspects have gone in, they'll have arrested them before she gets there, won't they?"

"That's the plan, even though that will mean they only have them on unlawful entry. The idea is then to set about proving it has to be this pair doing the murders."

"But?"

"It would be much better to actually catch them in the act, and I have a suspicion that Miller might quietly be planning to let her go in before they all charge in after her."

"They wouldn't do that, would they? Jayne could be hurt. I can't imagine the super would agree to it."

"He wouldn't, and I hope it's not what they intend to do."

Callie thought back to the briefing; when it had ended and people were leaving, Miller had called a few of them to stay behind, including Jayne. She wondered if any alternative plans had been discussed, ones that weren't for public consumption. She hoped not; she didn't want her friend to be put in any danger, even if it was to catch a killer, or killers.

"Have you had a chance to find out more about the marks?" she asked him.

"Yes," he sounded smug. "I rather think I know what they are."

"Well, come on then, spill the beans."

"It's the Kama Sutra."

"What?"

He explained that the Kama Sutra was not only about sexual positions and that it described ways of touching, hurting, hitting and biting and laid them down in different levels or degrees.

"Marking with the nails is one of the sections. It starts with 'sounding' when you touch your lover without leaving a mark, then there's the half-moon."

"Where you leave a half-moon shape from one nail."

"Exactly, then it's the circle, the line, the tiger's claw."

"That's the curve of five half-moons that Kate had," Callie couldn't help but shudder as she thought of that.

"Yes. You can also vary the meaning of the marks by changing where you leave them, and how deep they are."

"And how many more of these levels are there?" Callie asked, because that might give them a clue as to how many more deaths were planned, she thought.

"Um, three."

"Which are?"

"There's the peacock's foot, the jump of a hare and the leaf of a blue lotus."

"I can't wait to see those," she said sarcastically, and Billy knew to say nothing as she thought about what he had said. She wasn't sure it helped them at all with finding who was doing this.

"Maybe one of them is trying to tell us something."

"Like what?"

"That this is sexual, rather than just violence?"

"The marking is supposed to show depth of love and commitment."

"So perhaps it's about their relationship, and not really anything to do with the victims themselves."

"It makes a strange sort of warped sense."

"If you ever feel tempted to leave me a marked body as a show of affection, please don't."

Billy laughed.

"No problem. Will you tell Miller?" Billy asked.

"Yes, I think I should, don't you?"

"Yes, you have to, but just be ready for Bob Jeffries' response."

"I can hardly wait," she groaned.

Neither said anything for a few moments, finding comfort in just knowing the other was there at the other end of the phone line.

"Have you had a chance to look at that job advert I sent you?" Billy finally asked.

"Not yet," Callie replied quickly, "but I will, I promise."

"They are a nice bunch. You'd like them, I'm sure."

Callie wondered how he knew they were so nice. His role as a hospital pathologist didn't mean that he was in close contact with GPs, as a general rule, just those connected to the police. Perhaps he knew them from a social context? she wondered. Before she could ask any questions, Billy was saying his goodbyes and she was promising to be careful during the surveillance and also promising to contact the surgery in Belfast.

She looked up the Kama Sutra online, mentally reminding herself to clear her browsing history once she was finished and read up about the marks. There really wasn't much more to it than Billy had already told her, but at least it explained the jump up from three marks to five and meant she could stop wondering about a missed body somewhere.

Questions about her future kept running endlessly through her mind as she tried to sleep, until she finally got up, made herself a cup of tea and took out her laptop. Having googled the practice, she looked at the cheerful smiling faces of the staff. Billy was right, they did look a nice bunch. She downloaded the job application form and spent an hour or so filling it out.

Once done, she hesitated for a moment. She had the choice of saving the application to look at another day, or sending it in as complete. Finally, clicking on one of the buttons, she went back to bed, and this time, to sleep.

Chapter 25

"Hi," Callie said as she climbed into the back of the white Transit van parked outside the police station. She was a bit dismayed to see that there were only two seats in the back section, tucked behind the front seats, with some rather grubby-looking curtains that could be pulled across to screen anyone in the back from view. The set-up wasn't nearly as high tech as films and television had led her to believe it would be, and the thought of being in these cramped seats for a long time filled her with dread. Particularly as one of the seats was already taken by Bob Jeffries. Putting her medical bag further back and keeping hold of her tote bag, she sat on the remaining seat, having first inspected it for cleanliness. It just about passed.

"Evening," a young man in jeans and a sweatshirt turned and acknowledged her from the driver's seat.

Callie smiled and nodded to him in return.

"Dr Hughes, glad you could make it." Jeffries grinned. "Sorry it's not more comfortable, but I've chucked a load of cushions in the back so we can spread them out and take turns to lie on them for a break. You could always practice a few of the Kama Sutra positions if you're bored."

Callie groaned, she knew that telling him, and Miller, about Billy's discovery was a mistake, she just hoped the presence of others in the van would stop him going on about it too much.

She looked round at the odd assortment of dirty cushions and thought that it was unlikely she would take him up on the invitation.

The front passenger door opened and Abi Adeola got in. Dressed in plain clothes she looked stunning.

"Hiya," she greeted Callie, "just hitching a lift to the location. Hope you bought something to occupy yourself with you." She nodded at the tote bag Callie had on her lap.

"Of course." Callie had brought a Kindle, so that she could read without having to have a light on, some sandwiches, fruit, and a flask of coffee which she would try to make last as long as possible. She also had an empty wide-necked flask in case she really couldn't wait to go. She just hoped the others would look the other way if she needed to use it, and that she could trust them to keep looking away and not tell anyone about it afterwards. Now that she knew that Jeffries was in the van with her, she would need to be absolutely desperate to risk it.

Another man jumped in the van and sat on the floor, leaning against the back of Jeffries' seat.

"That's PC Cardle," Jeffries introduced him to Callie and he waved in her direction.

"Tom," he said pulling a cushion over to make himself more comfortable.

"The doc here can help with your position if you like." Jeffries couldn't help but giggle as he looked at Callie's horrified expression. Fortunately, PC Cardle didn't seem to know what he was talking about, that, or he was a very good poker player.

The back door was closed and PC Cardle pulled another curtain across it. Callie assumed that was so no one would be able to see in if they had to open the back door for any reason. Jeffries pulled the curtains between the front and back across too. They could not be seen in the back now, but would be able to look out by moving the curtain, or poking the lens of a camera through.

"Right, let's get going. We want to be in position well before Jayne gets there," Jeffries said once he was satisfied with the position of the curtains.

Callie did up her seat belt as the driver started the engine.

"Everyone okay back there?" Abi asked.

"Fine, thanks," Callie said and hoped she sounded like she meant it. As the van moved off, Cardle hung on to a strap hanging from the side of the van to stop himself from sliding around. Callie was glad she did at least have a seat.

It was going to be a long evening.

* * *

Once they were parked in a position where they could clearly see the entrance to the terraced house, Abi and the driver got out and walked away, chatting to each other and with not so much as a parting wave because they were being very strict about playing their parts and not giving anything away. As they headed off towards the pub where they were due to meet Jayne later that evening, Jeffries cautiously peeked through the curtain. Although it was still light outside, the back of the van was very dark. Cardle was busy playing with his very professional-looking camera and Callie realised he would need her seat once the surveillance started.

"Here, I'll move out of your way," she said and stood up.

"Cheers," he replied and they swapped places, with Callie stacking up a few of the elderly and dusty cushions. The lack of light meant she couldn't see the dirt, but the musty smell told her just how grim they probably were. With a slight shudder she sat on them and managed to make herself a reasonably comfortable seat leaning against the side wall of the van. There were a few ridges that dug into her back, but she wriggled around until they weren't digging in too much, and took out her Kindle. She was reading the latest Kathy Reichs and it was a bit of a luxury to have some uninterrupted reading time, if only Jeffries could be as quiet as his colleague. He had an earpiece in place and was obviously getting regular updates from elsewhere, which he then passed on to her and Cardle in a whisper. Actually, Cardle also had an earpiece in situ, Callie noticed, so Jeffries was presumably just telling her what was happening, which was nice, but interrupted her reading.

"They've got to the pub," he whispered to her.

She nodded. He began to look through the curtain more often and Callie could see that the light outside was fading fast. He elbowed Cardle in the ribs and the constable leant forward, pushing the camera through the curtains, and started taking photographs.

"Target one entering location one," Jeffries whispered into his microphone. "Jayne's just gone into the house," he interpreted for Callie.

"Okay," she whispered back, mindful of the fact that it was so dark now that he wouldn't be able to see if she nodded, and went back to her book, reading the same page again.

"Target one leaving location one," Bob whispered, as Cardle again photographed what was happening.

Once Jayne was out of sight, the two policemen continued to keep watch through the curtain, waiting for any sign of the killers.

Callie went back to her book, but every few minutes she was interrupted by Jeffries reporting that it was all quiet or that the other watchers, at the back of the house, were also reporting that nothing was happening.

Callie sighed. If she was honest with herself, it wasn't just Jeffries' interruptions that were stopping her reading, it was the tension. Her mind kept wandering off, thinking about what might happen; despite the book being very good, she'd reread the same page three times already.

Callie took out her sandwiches, and offered them round. Both Jeffries and Cardle accepted one, although Jeffries did sniff it suspiciously before deciding it was okay and eating it. Presumably he was worried she might have secreted some sort of vegetable in with the ham and mustard. Rather than offer them again, she just left the container in easy reach and the two men happily ate their way through them whilst Callie ate an apple, neatly placing the core in the empty sandwich wrapper and putting them back in her bag. Cardle and Jeffries had also both brought a variety of snacks, which they ate before dumping the wrappers on the floor, all the time keeping a close watch on the front of the house. They also shared a flask of tea Cardle had brought along. He offered Callie a cup, but she declined, still anxious about needing to pee later.

She went back to her book and managed to stop listening to Jeffries' updates for a while and read several chapters, until her bladder began to cause her concern. She was sure she didn't really need to go, but once the thought had entered her head she couldn't think of anything else.

Callie looked at the time on her phone. Only an hour and a half had gone by since Jayne had left the house; it felt much, much more than that.

"How long is she going to stay at the pub?" she whispered to Jeffries.

"Two hours or so the guv said, so she should be heading back here in a while," he whispered back. "If you need a piss, just head to the back of the van, have you got a bottle or something?"

"No, no, it's okay," she lied. "I'm fine." She was nowhere near desperate enough to do that.

The time really dragged after that and Callie was unable to concentrate on reading at all. She could feel the rising frustration as nothing happened with the house, plus she really couldn't stop thinking about how full her bladder was fast becoming and it was a relief when Jeffries reported that Jayne was leaving the pub and making her way back to the location. She was sure she could hold on for a little while longer, and magically the need to go disappeared now that she knew the wait would soon be over.

She heard the clicking noise of Cardle taking photographs as Jayne returned to the house and went in. A short while later, Abi and the van driver got in.

"The order is to stand down," Jeffries told her, although she had gathered that was the case. "Debrief at the station."

"What about Jayne?"

"She's going out the back to meet up with the lads there and go back with them."

Callie was relieved it was over and nothing had happened, but she had to admit that she really wasn't looking forward to having to do it all over again the next night, or even following weekend.

Chapter 26

On Saturday afternoon, Callie took a further look at her job application, but again hesitated to send it. She told herself it was because she wanted to get it absolutely right. She felt agitated and wasn't sure if it was the thought of another night in the surveillance van, or making the decision about her future.

When in doubt, clean something, had always been Callie's mantra, and putting together a collection of clothes and cleaning products, she slipped on her rubber gloves and set about the flat. She found that housework was a good way of emptying her head and letting her subconscious make the decisions. By the time she had dusted, vacuumed, and used plenty of bleach in the bathroom, she had made up her mind. She returned to her online application, read it through one more time, and pressed send. Job done.

* * *

That evening was a rerun of the night before: same surveillance van, with the same people. Abi and the driver going to the pub, leaving her, Cardle and Jeffries to wait in the van.

"Target one leaving location one," Jeffries whispered as Jayne once again went out to join her friends in the pub.

Callie would have dearly loved to join her. The cushions didn't seem nearly so soft the second night in a row. She wriggled and tried to get comfortable.

"What are the chances of us getting the right location first time?" she asked, in a whisper, of no one in particular.

"Don't even think about it," Jeffries said through a mouthful of her cheese sandwiches. "Not sure the super will let us do this again at another location. Not to mention that none of them are as good as this one from the surveillance point of view."

She dreaded to think how bad the others were, given that this one wasn't exactly ideal, considering its escape route onto the railway line. They waited tensely for something to happen, for someone to approach the door, or for news from those watching the rear of the house that someone was breaking in from there, but there was nothing, and the disappointment grew with every passing minute.

Callie leant back with a sigh and tried to concentrate on her book. This time she did manage to get into it, losing herself in the mystery and the Carolina countryside for a while. It seemed only a short time later that Jeffries piped up again.

"Target one returning to location one."

And then:

"Stand down, everyone, back to base for a debrief."

And absolutely nothing had happened.

The Peacock's Foot and The Jump of a Hare

It had been a long wait in the bedroom of the small house, but finally they heard the door open as someone came into the building. They heard her stumble slightly as she took off her coat and then giggle.

"Bloody thing!" she said sounding drunk and there was a rustle as she dumped the coat on the floor, then more footsteps as she made her way across the living room.

"Stop that!" she said and they listened.

Had she been talking to herself? There was some more rustling.

"No, just wait," she said.

Then what was unmistakeably a man's voice replied, "You're enjoying it really."

"Yes, but I need to have some coffee."

She went into the kitchen and there was some clinking and the sound of the tap running.

They looked at each other and then around the room. There was nothing they could do; it was too late to leave. They would have to get past the man and the woman downstairs in order to get out. Their best bet was to stay put. She shuddered, the thought that this time they could lose, that they could be hurt or killed themselves, made it so much more exciting.

"Where's the bathroom?" the man downstairs called to the woman who was making the coffee. Everything they were doing could be heard clearly in the bedroom above.

"Upstairs," she replied.

In the bedroom, they both tensed as the stair light was switched on, and again looked at each other in the small amount of light that was coming under the bedroom door. It had always been inevitable that despite all their planning, one of their targets would eventually bring someone back with them.

Perhaps they should have followed her to the bar or whatever, and then back from her night out? Like they had with the man in the flat – but they had discussed it and agreed that it would add a layer of risk. Risk of being seen, that is, of being caught on CCTV, and they had decided it wasn't worth it. However, now they had a whole new complication: two people to overpower.

From the sound of it, the woman wouldn't be too hard – she was drunk – but they had no idea how much of a problem the man would be. Perhaps he wouldn't expect to stay the night, or to take her to bed? Perhaps he would just have a nightcap or they might have sex downstairs. They both held their breath and didn't dare move in case they were heard as they listened to the heavy footsteps that came up the wooden stairs. The man was no lightweight, that was for sure. He went into the bathroom and the light went on. He didn't bother to close the door.

They heard a kettle going on downstairs as the man used the bathroom and then came out. He hesitated on the landing, and they held their breath. The door creaked as he pushed it further open, but after only a brief look into the bedroom, he went back downstairs again. He hadn't seen them.

They breathed again and silently reviewed their positions. He was behind the open door but she was on the other side of the room, hidden from view from the doorway by a large wooden wardrobe. She would be visible as soon as the first person came fully into the room. He indicated for her to move across to where he was. She very carefully moved, trying to be as quiet as possible, but her plastic overshoes rustled as she moved, and the old floorboards creaked.

"What was that?" asked the man downstairs.

"What?"

"I thought I heard something, someone moving upstairs."

In the bedroom, she froze where she was, halfway between the wardrobe and the safety of behind the door, not daring to breathe or move at all lest they heard her. One foot was raised slightly and she wobbled. She reached out to steady herself and grabbed the door handle. It rattled.

"Stay there!" the visitor said and then there was the sound of footsteps pounding up the stairs.

The woman smiled at her horrified lover: let the fun begin.

Chapter 27

"What have we got?" Callie asked as she approached the small post-war semi-detached house which, like its neighbours, had probably been a council house at one time. Most of the houses had almost certainly been sold and the owners were all desperate to make their homes seem individual. Where there had once been a unity in the short row of houses, some now sported porches of varying sorts, one had limestone cladding and another had pillars that would have looked over the top in a mansion. Everyone seemed to be trying to disguise their home's humble origins, and failing.

"Two bodies, upstairs bedroom," the constable at the door told her.

"Two?" she queried and hurriedly entered the house.

There was a short hallway with a door to the left, the stairs up to the second floor straight in front of her, and the kitchen at the back of the house. A coat was draped over the newel post, and a pair of small-size trainers had been kicked off and just left, one at the bottom of the stairs and the other halfway down the corridor to the kitchen. She leant into the living room to take a quick look. It was furnished in retro style, as befitted the age of the house. A larger coat had been neatly folded over the back of one of the chairs and a pair of very large trainers were placed neatly by the side of the sofa.

Callie walked along the edge of the short corridor to the small kitchen and peered in. A used coffee mug and glass in the sink, two cups out ready with instant coffee granules in them, a carton of milk, open, standing ready beside them, but nothing else out of place. She went back to the front door and up the stairs to a small landing where there was a bathroom and two bedrooms leading off it. She could see from the top of the stairs that the front bedroom was a scene of complete chaos. She thought it likely that the bodies were in there and moved to the doorway so that she could see.

There were shards of silvered glass all over the floor from a broken mirror, there was a blood-covered bedside lamp lying beside the bed. On the floor, partly covered by brightly patterned bedding, Callie could see a body. Judging by the size of the feet, she guessed the body belonged to a man. The woman was on the bed, fully dressed, lying on her back with her eyes wide open, staring at the ceiling. There was a thin scarf around her neck and signs that she had been strangled with it. She had bruising to her face, with blood around her nose and mouth. As Callie carefully moved a little closer, she could tell that the woman's nose was slightly bent, suggesting it had been broken – there was also a gash to her temple, but not much blood, she must have died soon after being hit. Her blouse, though still on, was pulled open and she could see some marks on the woman's left breast. Five individual nail marks, spaced out, like a bird's footprint.

"The peacock's foot," she said to herself.

Callie kept her examination of the two bodies to a minimum, she wanted to disturb things as little as possible, she simply needed to confirm death. She had to move some of the sheet from the man on the floor to do that, and she could see he was a fit-looking young black man in his thirties. He had a pool of blood under his head, and she thought that he had probably been hit by the table lamp lying close to his body. There were some marks on his breast too, but because of the dark tone of his skin, it was hard to see what they were, but she had a pretty good idea. She closed her eyes for a moment of contemplation and wished them both a peace in death that they had been denied in the minutes before dying.

When she carefully retraced her way outside, crime scene personnel were busy getting togged up, and a perimeter around the house had been taped out by additional officers. Miller and Jeffries were hurrying up the road and stopped beside her as she pulled back her hood and removed her mask.

"We got reports of two—" Jeffries started, before being interrupted by Miller.

"Is it them?" he asked anxiously. He looked terrible, as if he hadn't slept all night and, she couldn't help noticing, the clothes he had on looked very much like the ones he had been wearing at the debriefing the previous evening.

"I think so," she replied. "They both have the marks on their chests, like the others. But the killers probably weren't expecting two people to come back and these two put up a hell of a fight."

"That's something, at least," Miller replied.

She put a hand on his arm. "Are you—"

"Right!" Colin Brewer interrupted her as he joined them.

"Morning, Colin." Miller turned his attention to the older man. "We need you to throw everything at this. If the victims fought back, there must be some forensics for us, surely?" He sounded desperate and Callie could understand why.

"If there is anything there, we'll find it," Brewer replied confidently and headed towards the house. "Let's get some step plates down ASAP," he shouted to one of the CSIs who had nearly finished gearing up.

"How come this place wasn't on your list?" Callie asked Miller.

"I don't know," he said, tiredness etched in every line on his face. "But I will find out."

* * *

It wasn't until late that Sunday afternoon, when Callie was called in to the police station and made her way up to the incident room, that she managed to find out why the house had not been on the list of possible locations.

"The owners don't use any websites to advertise their place. They do it in a Facebook group."

"It means that they organise all the payments and bookings themselves," Nigel Nugent added from his desk, where he was still working through spreadsheets of information.

"So... which of our couples used them?" she asked.

"It's not as simple as that."

Of course not, Callie thought to herself; nothing about this pair is simple.

"We've got the owners in to interview them and get them to look at photos, but at the moment they are denying ever actually renting the place out."

"Let me guess," Callie said. "They aren't registered with the council or they don't declare their earnings for tax or something of that ilk."

"Both," Jayne said. "The boss is with them at the moment, and probably threatening them with the wrath of HMRC, not to mention the council enforcers. I'm pretty sure they'll crack and tell us who has rented it in the past pretty soon."

Callie sincerely hoped she was right.

"The victims probably felt they were safe renting the place despite the killings because it wasn't on any of the websites."

"Exactly," Jayne agreed, and added, smiling, "The good news is, the killers didn't succeed in a forensically clean kill, this time."

"Fantastic!" Callie would have done a little happy dance if she wasn't in the incident room, and there weren't so many people watching. Also, there really wasn't anything to dance about with two young people dead through no fault of their own.

"Yes, there's blood from several different donors, plus hair that doesn't match either of the victims, and multiple prints. It's going to be a nightmare to sort them all out, but with a bit of luck we'll have our killer's DNA in there somewhere."

"I sincerely hope so. What exactly did you want from me?"

"While we wait for the owners to come clean, we're bringing in all four of the suspects for interview and DNA samples, and we are hoping you can inspect them for any visible injuries as well."

"It will be a pleasure."

"If they agree to it."

"Well," Callie said, "if they are innocent, they will."

"And you never know," Jayne said, "the CPS might come back and say we can check them out whether they agree to it or not."

"That'll be a first, then."

Callie jumped, she hadn't heard Bob Jeffries come up behind her.

"One of the suspects has arrived and is downstairs," he told Callie. "The others are all on their way – well, two are – we haven't been able to get hold of one yet."

"What about the pair that were discounted because they hadn't booked anywhere else? Are they back in, now it looks like it was a private arrangement?"

"Fortunately for us, they both have alibis this time."

"But the ones you've called in haven't?"

He nodded.

Callie went over to the board displaying the pictures and details of the four people who, in pairs, were the only people still on the suspect list.

Sandy Lines, the receptionist at a beauty salon with Frederico Diaz, the engineer. A good-looking couple, well matched.

And below them, the blonde accountant from Crawley, Beth Jackson, with the grey civil servant from South London, Paul Langton.

"Which one is here?" Callie asked. "The one who lived in Crawley?" She tapped the photo of Beth; she was the person who lived closest, so it seemed logical.

"No," Jeffries said. "That's the one we haven't been able to get hold of yet. A Mr Rico short for Frederico Diaz, from South London, is in the interview room. The boss and I will interview him and see if he agrees to be examined and give us his DNA, if you want to get your set-up ready, Doc?"

Callie followed him down to the treatment room in the custody suite.

"What's your gut feel about Mr Diaz?" she asked.

"Only thing my gut can be relied on to tell me is when I'm hungry." He held a door for her and grinned. "But if I were a serial killer, I wouldn't voluntarily walk into a police station."

"These killers are pretty audacious."

"Yeah, but they must know they cocked up last night and it's only a matter of time before we pin it on them."

Callie considered this and knew that he was right. This couple were acutely forensically aware, so they would know the game was up. Would they run? Probably. She certainly would if she was one of them and she certainly wouldn't voluntarily walk into a police station and give them her DNA.

"That means, just by turning up, you think Mr Diaz isn't our man."

"Correct," he answered. "But all the more reason for us, and you, to prove it so we can concentrate on the real bastards."

There was no argument from her about that.

* * *

"Sit down please, Mr Diaz." Callie gestured to the chair set beside the examination couch. She was dressed in a forensic coverall, with gloves and overshoes on, just as she would be if she entered a crime scene. She had placed a series of packets on the couch in lieu of a work surface. "You have consented to be examined for injuries and to having a DNA swab taken for elimination purposes, is that correct?"

"Yes, of course. I have nothing to do with this. Please, do whatever you need to do to prove it." Mr Diaz seemed very anxious, but that was quite understandable given the circumstances.

Callie took a swab from the inside of his cheek, and placed it in a labelled tube and then into an envelope which she sealed. She then took a large sheet of paper and placed it on the floor.

"Please could you stand on the paper and remove your outer clothing."

Callie knew it was unlikely that even if he was the killer he was wearing the same clothes as he had during the attack, but after a discussion with the lab and Miller, it had been decided to act as if it was a possibility and Callie was to collect as much forensic evidence as possible. As Mr Diaz reluctantly removed each item of clothing, his mustard-coloured woollen jumper, white cotton shirt, smartly pressed jeans, and pristine trainers, he placed them in a large evidence bag she was holding out.

"When will these clothes be returned, please?" he asked, not unreasonably.

"I'm not going to lie, Mr Diaz, it's not likely to be for quite some time." If ever, she didn't add.

Once he was standing in nothing but his underpants, Callie looked closely at his body. There were no marks or scratches on the front half of his torso or legs and nothing but a small, fading bruise on the back of one calf, at least a few days old by the look of it. On instruction from her, he held out both hands, palms down, and she inspected them for scratches and then got him to turn his hands over so that she could look at the other side. There was nothing. She took scrapings from his fingernails, making sure the almost non-existent bits of dirt that she collected went into a small evidence bag that she then sealed.

"That's all fine, Mr Diaz, please get dressed now." She handed him the well-used, but clean, tracksuit and disposable slippers that were handed out to anyone who needed fresh clothing whilst they were in custody. He didn't seem overly happy with the choice, but realising it was that or drive home naked, he put them on.

"This has not been a good experience."

"I'm sure it hasn't, Mr Diaz, and I'm sorry for that." She was mindful that this man was almost certainly innocent simply by being there and allowing her to take these samples, and therefore it really was an imposition to take his clothes away, especially his almost brand-new trainers.

Once he had gone, she was told that Sandy Lines, the beautician from Croydon, had arrived. She was the other suspect, who, when considered along with Rico Diaz, had rented all the locations where the previous murders had taken place. Callie took great care to collect together all the samples and clothing she had taken from Mr Diaz, putting the bags into one large bag and handed it, along with a chart marking the only bruise visible on him, to Jayne. She didn't want there to be any question of cross-contamination.

"Didn't show any signs of recognition," Jayne said.

"Who?" Callie asked.

"Beautiful Sandy. I walked her in as Rico was being shown out, but neither of them gave any signs that they knew each other. It really doesn't look like they are our pair."

Callie didn't point out that if they were the killers and had taken great care to keep any connection hidden, they were unlikely to give the game away so easily.

"Any news on the other two?"

"He's on his way in, apparently, but we haven't been able to get hold of her. Local police are on their way to her address, to see if she's there."

Callie headed back to the treatment room, to make sure it was clean and ready for her next examinee. She had just finished laying out all the equipment she would need when there was a knock on the door.

"Hello?" she said as she opened the door to the young woman with a very cross expression who was waiting there with Jayne.

"Is this really necessary?" she asked and from the look on Jayne's face, and the short shrift she gave the question, not for the first time.

"Yes, now in you go," Jayne said.

Sandy scowled.

"Come in and take a seat, did they explain what I need to do?" Callie said.

"Well, this woman" – Sandy jerked her head at Jayne, who rolled her eyes at Callie – "she said I was to have my DNA taken to eliminate me, and I'm fine about that, but then she said you'd need to examine me for injuries and take my clothes for testing. I mean, they could've told me I'd need to leave my clothes, then I would have worn something I didn't care about. I mean, I ain't leaving these here, I'm telling you right now" – she indicated her high-heeled shoes and showed Callie the red soles – "they're genuine Louboutins, I ain't kidding ya. The real thing and they are not staying here with you lot, I'd never see them again, and I ain't going home in no used clothing, either. I got a thing about that, can't be wearing other people's stuff. No, no, no, I just can't do it."

"Okay." Callie held up a hand to stop the flow of complaints. "Jayne, can we forget about the shoes? I don't think it's likely anyone wore a pair of Louboutins to any of the scenes."

Jayne rolled her eyes again.

"Okay, I'll make a note of that and let them know."

Callie turned back to the young woman.

"And I'll give you a set of the coveralls we use at crime scenes to wear home – they're disposable so no one will have worn them before you," she told the woman, who visibly brightened.

"What? Like they wear on the telly? Cool!"

With a way forward agreed, Callie proceeded to examine and take samples from her.

The Leaf of a Blue Lotus

He cried when he told her he didn't want to get caught, that he couldn't face prison. She smiled at him, hugged him to her breast and made soothing noises as she stroked his head.

"Shh, I know," she said. "We have to run away."

"No!" He shook his head violently. "Our faces will be all over the press by tomorrow. Our names will be out there. We can't get away. Everyone is looking at us, and if they catch us, when they catch us, we will be sent to different prisons."

"We won't get caught."

"We will, and I can't bear to be apart from you," he said. He held her at arm's length and looked into her eyes. "If we kill ourselves, then we'll always be together," he said.

She knew he was right. The police would be looking for the two of them everywhere, and there wouldn't be much time before there was a knock on the door. Too late she realised that they should have planned for this. She nodded her acceptance.

He laid out all the items they would need. He took the pills that he had stolen from his mother's house when his father was dying, and piled them in the centre of the bed along with the two plastic bags to place over their heads when they were ready.

"It's for the best," he said and took her hand, leading her to the bed. He poured them both a tumbler of vodka and handed one to her. "At least this way we get to be together forever."

"Are you sure this is the only way?" she asked.

"Yes," he said simply and sat on the bed. "We have no choice."

She watched him as he began to take some tablets, swallowing them with the vodka. Then she sat down next to him, and began to do the same. When he began to feel sleepy he took the two bags and they both put them over their heads and sealed them. They lay down, side by side and waited to die. She fiddled with her bag, to make it more comfortable, she said, and reached out to touch him, pressing her nails into him, reinforcing her commitment to him as he began to lose consciousness.

Chapter 28

"I know she worked in a beauty salon, but how she managed to do anything with nails that long I don't know." Callie was in The Stag with Kate, sitting by the window, as their usual table had been taken by a group of tourists.

"Were they gels?"

"I suppose so – I'm not really up on fashions like that. I mean, doctors and nurses can't really have long fingernails – can you imagine trying to do an internal examination with nails that long?"

"Ugh, it makes you wince just thinking about it."

Kate took a drink of beer to banish the thought from her mind.

"Did all the suspects show up in the end?"

"No," Callie said, "just those two, which effectively rules them out."

"And effectively rules the other pair in."

"Yes."

"So, now it's just a case of finding them and that should be simple, even for the police."

Callie wondered if that was true. If it was so easy, she, and everyone else, would have heard by now. The silence from Miller and the lack of breaking news on the television must mean that they hadn't been located yet, let alone arrested. Callie knew that being called to attend the police station, having left the last scene in such a mess, would have alerted even the most stupid of criminals, and this pair were certainly not that.

"What would you do? If you had to disappear?" she asked Kate.

"Well, for a start, I would have left straight after that last killing to give me a head start. They would probably have hoped that no one would find the bodies for a day or two."

"Me too, but the man was still in the country, or at least still answering his phone, when they called to set up the elimination interviews."

"He might have been abroad."

"I think they would have noticed the different ring tone if so."

"Good point. And they've both gone silent now?"

"Yes. According to Jayne there was no sign of either of them at their addresses – they got local police to go around and check them out. Their phones are switched off– no!" She corrected herself, "One phone is switched off, hers – his is still on, but there's been no answer."

"They'll be able to find out where he is now, or rather, where his phone is."

"Yes," Callie answered. "But it takes time."

"And that is just what they need to get clean away."

"Exactly."

Even with a call-out to all ports and airports, things took time to filter through and she guessed that the pair were already abroad, phones ditched, new ones purchased, always supposing they didn't have more than one mobile phone from the beginning.

"This isn't going to end any time soon," Callie said. "It will take a while to find out where they've gone to."

"If they have done a runner already, we might never know."

Callie sincerely hoped her friend was wrong, but she knew it was realistic. This pair were planners, they would have had an escape route ready to go, she was sure. False passports and IDs would be hard to get hold of, but not impossible if you have the time, and they might have stocked up on spare phones, cash and maybe even know of somewhere they could stay, so they wouldn't need to use credit cards, withdraw money from their bank accounts, or show their passports, new or old, to check into a hotel — all different ways they could be tracked if they had left England, or even if they hadn't.

"You know, although it would be tempting to head out of the country, it's incredibly hard to keep under the radar forever. If you don't have vast amounts of cash, I mean."

"Hmm, that's true," Kate conceded.

"I think I would rent a place here for a few weeks, until things quietened down, if I were on the run."

Pictures of the two suspects, the same ones that Callie had seen pinned to the board in the incident room, had been featured on the evening news, with the usual caution for people not to approach the two of them but to call the number listed or 999 if they were spotted.

Beth Jackson, the accountant from Crawley, and grey-suited and serious-looking Paul Langton, the civil servant from South London. She wondered how they had met, what had drawn them together in the first place, and what had triggered them to start their killing spree.

"It wouldn't be any easier at a later date, though, would it?" Kate said. "There will still be electronic alerts on their passports and with their photos on every news programme. Someone will recognise them, surely? Even if they try and change their appearance."

Callie sincerely hoped she was right.

Chapter 29

Callie was still hoping that someone would recognise the pair quickly and she got up early to go to the incident room before starting work to see if there had been any news.

"They've found a body," Miller said as soon as she entered the room.

"Who found it?"

"The Crawley police broke into the female suspect's flat."

"He killed her," Callie said sadly.

"No," Jeffries replied. "She killed him. Or at least, let him die."

It took a moment for Callie to understand what he was saying, and another few seconds to believe it, but when she saw the full report it became clear. The death appeared to have been part of a suicide pact gone wrong.

Paul, the civil servant, had been found lying on the bed in the flat, apparently having taken a lot of pills. He had had a plastic bag tied around his head for good measure, in a manner that she knew was suggested and explained in detail on some suicide websites. There were marks on his breast, as with the other victims, in the shape of a lotus leaf as Callie had predicted the next victim would have.

There would be a post-mortem and his blood would be sent for toxicology tests to analyse the levels of the drugs, of course. Meanwhile, it was the pathologist's opinion that he had taken the drugs voluntarily, as there were no signs to the contrary, and that the number taken were probably enough to kill.

Looking at the review of external injuries, Callie saw that he had several recent bruises and scratches; nothing new enough to have been inflicted around the time of this death, but definitely less than a week old. It confirmed that his last two victims must have put up a vigorous fight.

"He sent a text message to his mother saying goodbye and asking her forgiveness at ten o'clock yesterday morning," Miller told her. "Judging by the spelling mistakes in that message, he was already affected by the pills he'd taken and the phone was found under the bed, as if he'd dropped it."

"What about the woman?" she asked.

"Her mobile was on the bed next to him, switched off. When our resident techy managed to get past the lock there were lots of missed calls from us, but no last-minute goodbyes or apologies from her." Jeffries sounded bitter.

"There was also a second plastic bag, and a half-drunk glass of vodka on the bedside table. And some tablets, some of which appeared to have been in someone's mouth and then spat out, were on the floor next to the bed." Miller just sounded tired and Callie gave him a concerned look, wondering if he had had any sleep at all in recent days.

"Maybe she changed her mind about going through with it," Callie said.

"Perhaps she never intended too," Jeffries responded. "Perhaps her plan was always to let him kill himself and then run away alone, knowing we would be looking for two people together. She is one smart lady."

"Kill her partner just to mislead us? That's cold."

"I think she's proved herself to be completely ruthless," Miller said. "And he may well have been at breaking point."

It certainly reversed what Callie had been thinking. She had assumed that the man had pushed and persuaded the woman to join him in killing people. That it was him who was the primary offender, but now, she had to consider whether it was her, the woman, who had led them into it.

"Do you really think she was the leader?"

Miller shrugged.

"With women? Anything is possible," Miller said and went into his office, closing the door behind him.

He clearly wanted some time alone and Callie wondered just what his current girlfriend had done to make him say something like that. But the more Callie thought about it, the more she understood how it might be true that Beth Jackson had been the leader of the pair.

She had been struck by the unlikely nature of the relationship between the tall, leggy blonde accountant and the rather pale, grey-suited, unsmiling civil servant. Now it seemed more understandable if perhaps she had been the one egging him on to do more and more risky things for excitement, culminating in the ultimate thrill, killing someone. He could have been so besotted by her that he would do anything for her, even kill, but then he had turned out to be the weaker link, a threat to her safety perhaps? And so she killed him.

Callie went up to the boards and examined the photographs, trying to imagine the pair as killers.

"It's a pretty horrific thought, isn't it?" Jayne was looking at her with concern.

"It's just awful, for a woman to do those dreadful things for, I don't know, for a thrill?" Callie was overwhelmed by the thought.

"Women are no better than men," Jeffries cut in. "The female of the species and all that."

But Callie couldn't believe he was completely right. Yes, women could be as violent as men, and in this case, certainly would seem to be, but in general, she told herself, she had to believe women were less likely to find killing an excitement, a means for self-gratification. There was a reason the vast majority of serial killers were men, wasn't there? And it couldn't be just because the female ones didn't get caught, could it? Surely not?

* * *

It was several days later and Callie had settled back into normal life. She had heard back from the practice in Belfast and planned to visit them and have an informal interview when she next went over to see Billy. There seemed no reason to go to the police station, until they asked her to come in and examine a prisoner who was claiming he had been beaten up when he was arrested.

When she checked him over, all she could find were a few bruises that were several days old, and some grazes to his knuckles that occurred when he had punched the arresting officer. Callie also examined the officer in question, a young woman who sported an impressive, and recent, black eye, but had no damage to her hands suggestive of hitting her arrestee back. She had more control than Callie, who would have been severely tempted to hit him back.

Having reassured the officer and the custody sergeant that all the evidence pointed to the prisoner having been the aggressor, not the officer, she took the opportunity to go up to the incident room to try and find out what was happening. Getting there, she was sad to see the room was being partially dismantled, even if she understood the reasons why: there were other crimes requiring attention.

"It's not as if she's likely to be in the area anymore, not if she's got any sense," Miller explained their position.

"We've collected and collated all the evidence. If she ever does reappear, we are confident we can nail her for the deaths," Jayne reassured her. "The DNA samples from her flat match those found at the last scene, along with his, of course."

"And we found their coveralls and stuff in the flats' communal bin," Jeffries added.

"Pretty clear cut then."

"Every police force in the country, Interpol, and the border force at all our ports and airports have been alerted to look out for her," Miller continued. "So now there is nothing we can do but wait for someone to find her."

"She's probably buggered off to some nice place to hide in the sun, Costa del Crime, or further afield, perhaps. It's what I would do." Jeffries looked almost wistful, as if he was wondering if he should just bugger off, hopefully without having to kill a bunch of people beforehand.

"So, there's nothing we can do but wait," Miller finished.

They seemed to be trying to reassure themselves as much as her, Callie thought.

* * *

"No news on finding this woman then?" Kate asked later that night in The Stag.

"Not a single sign of her anywhere," Callie replied.

"Perhaps she's killed herself."

"It's certainly a possibility, but somehow I don't think so. I mean, she had the chance to do that, when she was with her partner Paul, but she chickened out."

"Or never intended to go through with it in the first place."

"Indeed. In fact, I think you are absolutely right, there's something about her. She's so in control. It's like she's thought of everything."

"And she must have known in the initial rush to find them both, people were looking for a couple travelling together, so she was more likely to get away on her own."

"Yes, added to which, I get the impression that he might have panicked, if she was the driving force for their killing spree. His goodbye text to his mum showed remorse."

"What about hers?"

"She didn't bother to send any. There either wasn't anyone she wanted to say goodbye to, or she knew she wasn't going to die."

"There you go." Kate shook her head in admiration. "Like you said, she's a cool customer."

Callie took a sip of wine and thought for a few moments.

"But how is she living?"

"How do you mean?" Kate said.

"She can't access her bank accounts or credit cards because they are being monitored, so how is she paying for stuff?"

"Perhaps she had a wad of cash stowed away somewhere, just in case."

"Mmm, but that would have to be a lot, a pretty big stash, to keep her going until the heat goes down."

"Maybe she took out cards in other names?"

"That's incredibly hard to do, unless you set up a whole new identity, you know, like they always do in books, getting a birth certificate of someone who has died and using it to get a passport and so on. The police are looking into it, but to do something like that, and have it ready in case, that shows an incredible amount of forethought on her part."

"Like you said, she's a planner," Kate responded and took another sip of her drink. "What about facial recognition? I heard that they can do amazing things with that. If she's taken out a passport in another name, couldn't they use that to find out?"

"I'm sure Steve's trying all these things, and I hear what you're saying, that she's a planner, but I just can't believe she set such a complex escape route up from the start."

"Then, we're back to the beginning, how is she managing to evade capture for so long?"

It was something that Callie gave a great deal of thought to over the next few days.

Chapter 30

"Hi Steve," Callie said as soon as Miller answered his phone. "Are you still monitoring Paul Langton's bank accounts and credit cards?"

"Yes, of course."

"And?" she coaxed.

"And there's been no activity on them since his death."

"And that's all his cards, is it? Or just the ones that you found on him?"

"How do you mean?"

"I was thinking about how she was managing to live and I thought, what if she took a credit card with her, how would you know? I mean, if it was one from his bank, you would know that from them, but what if he had another one? I've got three cards, one for work-related things, you know, expenses I can claim back, and two to juggle if needed. He might even have another bank account to go with one. Have you checked?"

"I'm sure they have," he replied, without any great certainty, "but I promise I will get them to take another look in case. I'll get Nigel on to it straight away."

"Oh, and Steve?" she added before he could put the phone down. "It might be worth checking the same thing for all of the victims. It could take a while for relatives to put a stop to theirs, particularly if they don't really know what cards and accounts exist."

The more she thought about it, the more she was sure this was the way Beth Jackson was managing. If she hadn't yet got a new identity, and she wasn't using anything in her name, she had to be using other people's cards, cards that she had stolen. If they could find out whose, and trace some transactions down to her, they would at least know whereabouts in the country, or even which country, she was in.

* * *

When Callie finished her morning surgery and made her way up to the main office, she was surprised to see a huge bunch of flowers waiting for her.

"Who are these from?" she queried as she reached for the card that had come with them.

"Read the card," Linda said, a little impatiently.

"'Thank you for your help', and it's signed from Lewis Conway." Callie smiled. "That's nice of him." She had seen a brief report from the cardiologist saying that they had found an episodic arrythmia that had been causing Mrs Conway's 'falls' and that they had put in a pacemaker. She was being discharged back to the nursing home today, and Callie added her patient to her visit list. It was nice when she was able to solve a problem so easily.

"Always good to be appreciated," Linda said. "You haven't forgotten the practice meeting, have you? Dr Grantham wants everyone there."

"No, of course not." Although, of course, she had forgotten it.

She checked her watch; there was no time to do the visit to Mrs Conway now. It would be hard enough to get any of her paperwork done before the meeting, let alone do any visits. She hurried into the kitchen and made herself a cup of coffee – that was definitely her number one priority.

* * *

The room was packed with people and not just the usual medical, nursing and senior administrative staff who attended practice meetings. Callie had never seen so many of them all gathered together at the same time in one room, not even at the Christmas parties. This, more than anything, told her that Dr Grantham was going to be making a major announcement about something that affected them all.

"Thank you all for finding the time to come here, especially those of you who have come in on your own time." Dr Grantham nodded at Gauri, whose day off it should have been. "I'm sure it can't have escaped any of your notice that I have been missing from the surgery rather a lot lately. I'm sorry to have to tell you that my dear wife, Esme–" his voice broke slightly as he said her name and he took a moment to control himself "–Esme, has been diagnosed with stage 4B ovarian cancer."

There was a whisper of noise around the room as people shifted uncomfortably in their seats. Callie looked round, everyone looked shocked except for Gauri and Linda, who must both have known already, she concluded.

"I'm so sorry, Hugh–" Callie started to say, but he waved her response back and hurried on, probably because he knew he would never get to the end without breaking down completely if he didn't.

"I'm sure I don't have to tell most of you what that means, but this meeting isn't directly about her condition, but more about what I intend to do. Esme is about to start her first course of chemotherapy on Monday. This will be the start of a long and difficult journey for both of us, and I intend to be at her side every step of the way. She is, has to be, my priority. To that end, I have decided to step down as senior partner and take my retirement now."

There was more of a concerted outcry at this but Dr Grantham again hushed them.

"It would be unfair for me to continue trying to juggle my responsibilities when all I want to do is be with Esme. I need to concentrate every ounce of my energy on her. I do hope you all understand."

He paused for moment and Callie looked around the room; everyone appeared upset and there were a few tears. Esme had been an ever-present, unpaid member of staff for many years, making sure that birthdays weren't forgotten, buying flowers when they were what people needed, and standing at her husband's side at every practice party for as long as Callie could remember. She would be missed by them all and they were all silently wishing her well, however unlikely it was that she would recover.

"Now, I have decided that my role as senior partner here should be taken by Dr Sinha, Gauri, she is the longest serving member of our partnership and, I'm sure you will all agree, will make an excellent leader" – he nodded in Gauri's direction and she gave a little, embarrassed, smile of acknowledgement – "and I hope you will all give her all the support and help that you have given me over the years. Thank you."

He gestured for Gauri to stand and say a few words, and as she did so, he slipped away. Callie could understand why; he didn't want to hear the tearful well-wishing and outpouring of sympathy or endure the hugs and hand-holding that would accompany them. She would have been the same. Sometimes, people's kindness was the hardest thing to bear. He had said his goodbye, and now he just wanted to go, so she let him.

She would find the time to visit and speak to them both personally as soon as she could, and maybe she should write a letter, because, goodness only knew, it was going to be so very hard to find the right words.

Chapter 31

"It seems like the end of an era," she told Billy on the phone that night.

"Maybe it is," he responded and cleared his throat. "Um, and so maybe it's the right time to go."

She gave it some thought.

"Maybe, but equally it would seem a bit like I was deserting Gauri, after all, she's going to have−"

"Please," he cut in, tired and annoyed. "Please don't make this yet another excuse not to come and join me."

"It's not an excuse." Her voice was tight and angry. How dare he say that? "I'm just saying that I should wait a few weeks to hand in my notice. Give her a chance to get settled in."

"And what about the job here? You agreed to visit them and they are expecting you. They are waiting for you because they are so sure you are the right person."

"I've spoken to them and told them there's a delay and no, they weren't happy, but they did understand my reasons."

"Before speaking to me?"

"I wanted to know if it was possible to delay it before telling you." Callie left unsaid that she knew he'd try and talk her out of it unless it was a done deal.

"And I'm supposed to just accept your decision too?"

"I just want to make sure Gauri's settled in before I hand in my notice; after all, it's a big change." She rubbed the spot on her forehead where a sudden and intense pain spoke volumes about the tension and stress she was experiencing. "Look, we're both tired and this is maybe not the best time to discuss this, let's sleep on it and talk again tomorrow, when we've had a little time to think about it."

There was a silence at the other end of the line.

"Billy? I honestly love you, and want to be with you. I'm not pulling out, I just need a little more time."

And that's how they left it, Billy still upset by the delay but, she hoped, accepting that that was all it was, a delay, not the end of their relationship.

* * *

"And that is all it is?" Kate queried the next day over their regular brunch, leaning close to make sure she could be heard. "A delay?"

The café was crowded and they had been unable to get their usual table by the window so were right next to the kitchen area, which was noisier and the smell of fried food much stronger.

"Yes," Callie replied, perhaps more firmly than she felt. "I just want to give Gauri a bit of time to get herself sorted and settled before I go."

"Have you told her you plan to leave?"

"Not yet," Callie admitted. "I don't want to add to her problems at the moment. Recruiting a new partner is such a big thing to do."

Kate gave her a long look.

"And what about Billy?" she asked.

"I still plan to go to Northern Ireland, to be with him, just not right now."

"Are you sure? Or are you just trying to convince yourself that you still intend to go?"

Callie was saved from having to reply by her mobile phone ringing.

"Hello? ... Oh, hi, Jayne ... What? I can't hear you — just a moment."

There was a lot of noise coming from the busy kitchen and she moved outside so that she could hear what the police sergeant was saying. With a sigh, Kate reapplied herself to her breakfast.

Huddled in a doorway to keep out of the rain, Callie spoke again.

"Sorry, Jayne, it was a bit noisy in there. What's going on?"

"We've got her! Well, not actually physically but we know where she is!"

Jayne sounded understandably excited.

"Fantastic news, where?"

"Here! In Hastings! Would you believe it?"

Callie could, as she had thought it would be easier to stay hidden somewhere known to you, but where you weren't known in return. In Crawley the suspect would have risked being seen by someone she knew, but she had only been to Hastings as a visitor and to stake out possible kill sites. She didn't actually know anyone in the town so there was little risk of being recognised, so long as she had changed her appearance from the press photos.

"And how do you know she's there?"

"You were absolutely on the button when you told us to look at credit card activity. She must have taken a card from pretty much all of the victims; ones that weren't issued by their banks, so they hadn't been stopped."

"And the credit card companies hadn't either?"

"No. They hadn't been informed of the holder's death, unlike the bank, so why would they? None of the executors had noticed or got around to closing them down. Well, one had recently which helped because he told his local police that there had been a transaction attempt after he'd cancelled it and when he checked the account, he could see that there had been several transactions before that, but after his sister had died."

"And the local police hadn't told you?"

"No, I don't think they had even realised it was one of our victims until we put out a specific enquiry to the local police forces of each of the victims and someone twigged."

"Thank goodness they did. So, now that you know she's here, what are you going to do? Put out an alert?"

"Bit more than that. Nigel's analysed all the transactions and, much as she has been doing her best to vary the locations and her use of the cards – different supermarkets in different parts of town, that sort of thing – Nigel is pretty sure of the area where she is staying, and more than that" – she paused for effect – "he's pretty sure she is renting a room in a hostel near the station. She's used several different names and cards to pay there."

"Don't they notice that she's doing that?"

"It's not manned. You know, it's one of those places where you use a machine outside and when your card goes through, it gives you a unique code to open the hostel door and your room."

Callie couldn't help thinking it was a pity none of the holiday homes had utilised that sort of technology, but then no one anticipates a serial killer using their facilities.

"She must know that we will catch on eventually."

"Yes, so it's important we pick her up as quickly as possible, before she moves on." There was a shout in the background. "Gotta go, we've got a briefing on the op now. I just wanted to let you know."

"Thank you," Callie said to the air because Jayne had already gone.

Returning to her table, Callie told Kate about this development in a hushed whisper.

"Bloody good thing too." Kate had finished eating but Callie's plate was still half full. "Are you going to eat that?" Kate asked.

Callie was too excited to eat any more and pushed her plate away.

"No, it's a bit cold now."

"Just go." Kate smiled as she reached for another slice of toast.

"Go where?"

"To the station, so you can find out what's happening. I can tell that's what you want to do."

As usual, Kate was right.

"I'll stay here and finish your breakfast for you," she said to Callie's fast disappearing back.

Chapter 32

Callie thought she knew which hostel Jayne had meant when she told her where Beth Jackson was hiding out. What was more, she knew she could easily walk past it on her way to the police station. The rain had temporarily stopped but she kept her umbrella ready in case. Although she felt she knew the killer well, having seen her photograph and the information gleaned from social media, they had never met in person – as far as Callie knew, anyway. There was no reason for the woman to have any idea who Callie was, so she felt it was safe to go past the place, and she could always put up her umbrella just to be sure she wasn't recognised.

As she walked up the road from the shopping centre, heading towards the railway station, she started looking to see if she could spot any of the police officers that she knew must be watching the hostel. Seeing none, she crossed the road and walked past the new college buildings to where she thought the hostel was, and found it easily. It had presumably been built at the same time as the college when the whole station approach area had been developed a few years earlier.

The college and hostel buildings formed part of a pedestrianised plaza, along with a restaurant, some offices, a medical centre and pharmacy. Unfortunately for the police, there was nowhere you could park a car or easily hang around without attracting attention, which must be making the stakeout a nightmare, she thought. Looking at the position of the hostel, the last building before the rail tracks, the police would be able to watch the back from the station platforms, she thought, but the front was much harder.

She paused and looked around her, as if she was trying to get her bearings. The hostel door was closed and she could see that it had an electronic lock that only those with a key card could open. She wondered whether Miller had managed to get hold of the company and get a card to enter the building, or if they were going to wait for the suspect to leave and grab her then.

Callie had deliberately not paused directly outside the entrance to the hostel, and was trying her best to look as though she was not paying it any special attention – that she was actually more interested in finding something else.

She walked past the entrance and towards the convenience store taking up the ground floor of the college building. She was heading back in the direction of the bus stops and took a good look around, trying to spot anyone that she thought might be from the police.

She saw one of the constables who had been at the stakeout briefings sitting on a bench by the bus station, smoking a cigarette. Then she spotted Jayne standing outside the train station café, protected from the worst of the weather by the building itself. She was holding a takeaway cup of something hot and seemed to be trying to look as though she was waiting for someone.

"Hello, Jayne." Callie came up and spoke to her, hoping that she just looked like the person Jayne had been waiting for.

"What are you doing here?" Jayne asked crossly but with a smile that would hopefully make it look as though she was welcoming her friend, in case she was being watched.

"Just thought I'd see how things were going. Is she in there?" Callie deliberately didn't look at the building.

"We believe so, but you really shouldn't be here."

"You didn't honestly think I'd keep away when you told me where she was, did you?"

"The boss will have my guts for garters."

"How will he know?"

"He's watching from the college building where they've set up a base. Fortunately the college is closed today," Jayne answered, before putting her hand up and touching her ear.

Callie could see she had an earbud in and then she touched the wire leading down to her phone.

"Yes, Bob. She's just happened to be passing and is leaving now." Jayne muted her phone mike. "The boss isn't amused."

"So I gathered. I suppose I can't wave to him." She gave Jayne an impish grin.

"Don't you dare – he really would have a stroke."

"Hm, don't tempt me."

"You know he's split up with her, don't you?"

"The girlfriend?"

Jayne nodded.

"She dumped him for a corporate lawyer with a sports car."

"That tells you everything you need to know about her."

"Quite. He was pretty cut up about it though."

Jayne was once again distracted by the conversation she was hearing through her earbuds and then reached to unmute her mike again.

"Yes, okay, I'll send her up." She turned to Callie. "The boss wants you to go up and be with them in the college office. I don't think he trusts you to keep away. Go in the main entrance and up to the first floor. The room's marked 'Media Studies' and for God's sake don't tell him it was me who told you where we were."

"I promise," Callie reassured her before giving her a little wave and hurrying over to the college building.

Inside the front entrance she saw three other police officers sitting around the unmanned reception area, waiting for an alert telling them the suspect was outside. They looked up briefly as she came in and then returned to examining their phones. What did people do when they had to wait around before the advent of smartphones? Callie thought as she made her way up the stairs to the first floor and found herself in a corridor with multiple doors leading off on both sides.

Once away from the main stairwell, the light was bad and it was hard to see the names on the doors. She guessed it would be a door to her left as that was the direction which would overlook the plaza, and three doors along, she came to one she was pretty sure said 'Media Studies'. She paused, unsure whether she should just go in or knock first. It opened before she had a chance to do either.

"Watcha, Doc," Jeffries greeted her and held the door open so that she could enter.

"What the bloody hell do you think you're doing, turning up at an operation like this?" Miller demanded as she came into the room.

"Good morning, or rather" – she looked at her watch – "good afternoon. It's nice to see you too." She gave him a smile, but he wasn't amused, she could tell.

Jeffries had taken up a position by the window and was looking out through the half-open Venetian blinds.

"This isn't the time or place for amateurs," Miller said, angrily.

"I am not an amateur," she replied coldly. "Can I remind you that I work for the police and that I was part of the stakeout only last weekend."

"When you were asked to be there by myself, and I was clearly wrong to do so," he snapped back. "So kindly keep out of the—"

There was a burst of static.

"Door opening," came from the radio on the desk beside Miller.

"Boss!" Jeffries said urgently.

Miller jerked round and looked out of the window. Callie moved forward too, so that she could see what was happening. Looking between the slats of the blind, there was a clear view of the hostel entrance. The door was opening and a young black woman came out.

Callie hadn't been aware that she was holding her breath but she let it out with a sigh and realised that the others were too.

"Not our target," Jeffries said into the radio, letting the others know to stand down. "Repeat, not target."

"Anyway, now that I am here, can I stay?" Callie asked. "Just for a while."

"I suppose so," Miller said grudgingly. "So long as you keep out of the way."

Callie pulled a chair closer to the window and moved the blind a little so that she could see better. She sat herself down at an angle to the window, so that it didn't look like she was watching the plaza if anyone was checking from the building opposite, but it did mean that she still had a good view of whatever was happening. Which was currently very little.

Callie took a good look at the hostel windows. Unsurprisingly, given the inclement weather, all of the windows were closed. With one or two exceptions, most of the windows had their main curtains open but it was still difficult to see into the rooms unless the lights were on.

"Do we know which room she's in?"

"Round the back, overlooking the railway tracks," Jeffries told her. "Curtains are still drawn so we can't see if she's there."

This meant there was little or no risk of them being watched from one of the windows opposite, and Callie didn't need to be quite so cautious about being spotted. She leant forward for a better look around the area. Jayne was chatting to another female detective by the train station door; the constable who had been sitting by the bus stop had moved away, but Callie was pretty sure a man looking at the bus timetables was another police officer.

"Cuppa, Doc?" Jeffries asked.

"No thanks, I've just eaten an enormous breakfast," she replied, not entirely truthfully, but she didn't want a cup of instant coffee and sterilised milk which was all she thought would be on offer.

"Toilets are at the end of the corridor by the stairs," Jeffries continued to keep her informed as he poured himself a mug of tea from a flask, "should you need them."

Of course Callie hadn't needed them until he mentioned it, but now? He had a habit of making her want to go but she told herself firmly not to be so silly and went back to watching the door and the people making their way to the railway station.

There was a woman struggling with her shopping bags and two young children, an elderly man stumbling slightly as he got off a bus, a young man with his eyes glued to his mobile phone who almost bumped into a lamppost.

She jumped as there was a crackle of static again.

"Door opening."

She watched the hostel door open and a group of young people, all dressed in torn jeans, trainers and baseball caps came out, laughing and joking.

"Not her," Miller said into the radio and they all breathed out again.

Jeffries handed Miller a mug of tea and started digging around, looking for a biscuit in the supermarket carrier bag on the desk. Callie continued to watch the group of young people as they walked across the plaza. One of them was doing a little dance to music only she could hear and the others teased her. The girl at the back was lagging behind slightly and as she went to pull her baseball cap down further, she turned slightly.

"It's her!" Callie shouted and dashed to the door. "Last girl in that group!"

Miller and Jeffries looked out of the window trying to confirm what she said.

As she ran to the stairs she heard Miller shout into the radio.

"Last female in that group of kids that just came out. Can someone stop and check that she isn't our suspect, repeat, the last female in the group, please stop and check!"

Callie ran down the stairs two at a time, and saw the three police officers who had been in the reception area get to the front door before her and rush out. Once outside she had the advantage over them in that she knew in which direction the group had been walking and dancing and what the person with them looked like. It was the fact that the last girl was older than the others that had first alerted Callie's subconscious, telling her that the woman didn't fit with the group of teenagers. Callie raced towards the shopping centre, aware that the three police officers, who were still looking in the wrong direction, wouldn't be far behind her. Jayne and others were hurrying across from the station but were still some way back. She hoped she had been right about the last person being the suspect, if not, she had just made sure everyone in the area knew the police were watching the hostel, that was for sure.

As she reached the road, the traffic lights were against her, but she could still see the group, including Beth

Jackson, walking down the hill towards Priory Meadows. If they got to the shopping centre it would be way too easy for the suspect to just leave the group and disappear into the crowds. Callie knew she had to stop that from happening and dashed across the road, only just missing being hit by a taxi. The driver had to brake sharply, but fortunately didn't use his horn which might have alerted the group that they were being followed. Callie wasn't worried about most of them knowing, they were so engrossed in their chatting she was pretty sure they didn't even realise they had an extra person tagging along, she was only worried about the woman at the back being alerted.

As Callie jogged quickly down the hill, trying to look like nothing more than a woman in a hurry, Beth Jackson was keeping her head down and walking swiftly. There was a loud blare of a horn behind Callie and Jackson turned, looking over her shoulder, as did Callie. The three burly police officers from reception had followed Callie across the road against the lights, but were less successful at being discreet. Realising that they were almost certainly after her, Jackson broke into a run.

Cursing silently, Callie did too.

The suspect ran past Primark into the pedestrianised square with Callie in hot pursuit. Behind her, Callie could hear the pounding of feet that meant that the others weren't far behind her.

"Stop! Police!" one of them shouted, but Jackson, and Callie, kept on going.

She wasn't far behind now and, thinking that they were making for the road, she started to cut the corner to close the space between them further, but at the last minute, Jackson changed direction and ducked into the shopping mall.

Callie swung left and had to dodge a woman with a pushchair and toddler in tow. Behind her she heard a crash and a shout and saw that one of the police followers had not managed to avoid them and had sent the mother, and himself, flying. The toddler was screaming and the pushchair was upended.

She hesitated, should she stop and make sure they were all right? She was a doctor after all, but other people were helping and she could see Jayne and others not far behind, so, after only a moment of hesitation, she left them to deal with it and went into the shopping centre.

She ran forward, trying to check shops as she went past, some of them further into the centre had more than one entrance, and exit, and she didn't want her prey to dodge through and out the other side.

"Mind out, will ya!" was shouted by someone ahead of her, then "What's the fucking hurry, love!"

Callie sprang forward, sure that it must have been Jackson they were complaining about, and as she reached the end of the main drag, she saw the woman ahead, running towards Marks and Spencer, which Callie knew for certain had a second exit. She could only hope that as she was simply a visitor, the woman wouldn't be aware of it.

Sure enough, rather than go into the shop and possibly get trapped, Jackson turned right and headed for the main shopping centre exit, with Callie just a few paces behind her. As Jackson reached the wall of doors, a police car screeched to a stop in the road outside, and two officers flew out of it and towards the entrance. Jackson turned and faced Callie who stopped as well. They were both breathing heavily.

"It's over," Callie said, sounding calmer than she felt. "Give yourself up."

Instead, Jackson let out a roar of rage and charged towards Callie, who felt herself pushed out of the way as one of the police officers rugby-tackled their suspect and brought her to the ground. Much to Callie's relief, by the time she had picked herself up, Jackson was safely in handcuffs.

Jayne and some of the others belatedly arrived, all breathing heavily after their exertions, and finally there was Miller. He approached the handcuffed woman and removed her baseball cap. Her hair was much shorter than it had been in her photo, not to mention a different colour, but she was still unmistakeably the same person.

"Beth Jackson, I am arresting you on suspicion of murder, you do not have to say anything, but it may harm your defence if you do not mention when questioned something which you later rely on in court."

A crowd had gathered, watching closely and listening to every word. Callie was pretty sure someone would be recording it on their mobile phone as well; she just hoped they hadn't managed to film her facing the suspect, or being unceremoniously pushed out of the way. Sure enough, as the suspect was led away towards the waiting police car, Callie could see several people filming the event and there was a smattering of applause as some of the crowd realised that this might be the arrest of the killer they had heard about on the news.

Once it was all over, Bob Jeffries finally arrived, bright red in the face and gasping. He bent forward, hands on knees, trying to get his breath.

"Nice of you to join us, Bob," Miller said and a few of the others smirked. "Right, let's get back and start making our case."

As they all started leaving, Miller turned to Callie.

"Good job," he said and smiled at her. For Miller, that was high praise.

"Yeah," Jeffries added, beginning to get back to the right colour. "Good thing you were there, Doc."

Callie couldn't stop grinning as she walked all the way home.

Chapter 33

Back at her flat, Callie had a long hot shower and resolved to go to the gym more often. Even though the chase hadn't been over a long distance, she had felt it, although probably not as much as Bob Jeffries had.

"I thought he was going to have a heart attack," she told Kate on the phone later. "He was beetroot-coloured and gasping for breath."

"I can't tell you how much of a relief it is to know that the woman's been caught. I can't believe she had stayed in the area."

"I don't think she was planning on being around much longer," Callie said. "According to Jayne they found several birth certificates in her handbag, all from local people who would have been around her age but had died in childhood."

"You think she was planning on using them to get passports?"

"Yes, and then she would have been able to go abroad, or maybe start again under a new identity here."

"Blimey, good thing you spotted her then."

"I was lucky," Callie admitted. "If she hadn't looked up and been so obviously older, I wouldn't have thought twice about her being one of the group. Mind you, if she'd gone back to her place later they would probably have spotted her then, anyway."

"But what if she didn't? What if she'd clocked that the place was being watched and wasn't intending on going back? It doesn't bear thinking about."

Callie knew she was right. They could so have easily missed Jackson, and once she had received one of the fake passports, she could open a bank account, apply for credit cards, get a National Insurance number, a job even. She had been only one short step from having a completely new identity. She had been so close to getting away with it.

Later, she phoned Billy to tell him about it.

"Once she was under arrest, I left them to do all the boring bits. After all, they have loads of evidence, even if she doesn't talk, and I fully expect her not to at this stage. There's no way she's going anywhere, any time soon."

"Well, that's a relief," he answered, but he wasn't as excited as her. In fact, he seemed a bit subdued.

"I will be coming over, Billy, I promise." Callie sensed that he was still upset about her not handing in her notice. "I'll speak to Gauri tomorrow, tell her that I'm planning to leave as soon as she's settled."

"You know, you have to give six months' notice, so you could hand in your resignation tomorrow, and she will still have those six months to find your replacement."

"Yes, but it will probably take longer than that for Gauri to find someone, you know that. I'd rather give her a bit a longer."

"The surgery here won't wait forever."

Callie hesitated before replying. It sounded as if Billy was saying that he wouldn't wait forever.

"There will be other jobs, Billy," she said quietly. "You know that."

"I know, it's just that I miss you."

"And I miss you, but you just need to give me time."

They finished the conversation on a more intimate note but Callie couldn't help wondering if she was pushing Billy too far, expecting him to wait so long, not even giving him a date to work towards. Well, she'd find out soon enough, she thought, and there was, perhaps, just a teeny little bit of her that wanted him to break up with her, take the decision out of her hands so that she didn't have to leave her home and her friends and start again, even to be with the man she loved.

THE END

If you enjoyed this book, please let others know by leaving a quick review on Amazon. Also, if you spot anything untoward in the paperback, get in touch. We strive for the best quality and appreciate reader feedback.

editor@thebookfolks.com

www.thebookfolks.com

ALSO IN THIS SERIES

Available on Kindle and in paperback.

DEAD PRETTY – Book 1

When a woman is found dead in Hastings, Sussex, the
medical examiner feels a murder has taken place. Yet she
feels the police are not doing enough because the victim is
a prostitute. Dr Callie Hughes will conduct her own
investigation, no matter the danger.

BODY HEAT – Book 2

A series of deadly arson attacks piques the curiosity of
Hastings police doctor Callie Hughes. Faced with police
incompetence, once again she tries to find the killer
herself, but her meddling won't win her any favours and in
fact puts her in a compromising position.

GUILTY PARTY – Book 3

A lawyer in a twist at his home. Another dead in a private pool. Someone has targeted powerful individuals in the coastal town of Hastings. Dr Callie Hughes uses her medical expertise to find the guilty party.

VITAL SIGNS – Book 4

When bodies of migrants begin to wash up on the Sussex coast, police doctor Callie Hughes has the unenviable task of inspecting them. But one body stands out to her as different. Convinced that finding the victim's identity will help crack the people smuggling ring, she decides to start her own investigation.

DEADLY REMEDIES – Book 5

When two elderly individuals pass away, it is not an unusual occurrence for seaside town doctor and medical examiner Callie Hughes. But she notices that both of the deceased had a suitcase packed, and her suspicions are aroused. Who is the killer that is prematurely taking them to their final destination?

OTHER TITLES OF INTEREST

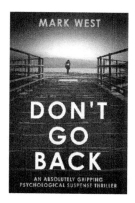

Gripping debut psychological fiction by Mark West

Beth's partner Nick can't quite understand why she acts so strangely when they return to her hometown for the funeral of a once-close friend. But she hasn't told him everything about her past. Memories of one terrible summer will come flooding back to her. And with them, violence and revenge.

The debut cozy Scottish mystery by Traude Ailinger

After being nearly hit by a car, fashion journalist Amy
Thornton decides to visit the driver, who ends up in
hospital after evading her. Curious about this strange man
she becomes convinced she's unveiled a murder plot. But
it won't be so easy to persuade Scottish detective DI
Russell McCord.

For more great books, visit www.thebookfolks.com

Printed in Great Britain
by Amazon

83683979R00133